This Is the End

This Is the End
Stella Benson

MINT EDITIONS

This Is the End was first published in 1917.

This edition published by Mint Editions 2021.

ISBN 9781513291161 | E-ISBN 9781513294018

Published by Mint Editions®

MINT
EDITIONS

minteditionbooks.com

Publishing Director: Jennifer Newens
Design & Production: Rachel Lopez Metzger
Project Manager: Micaela Clark
Typesetting: Westchester Publishing Services

This is the end, for the moment, of all my thinking, this is my unfinal conclusion. There is no reason in tangible things, and no system in the ordinary ways of the world. Hands were made to grope, and feet to stumble, and the only things you may count on are the unaccountable things. System is a fairy and a dream, you never find system where or when you expect it. There are no reasons except reasons you and I don't know.

I should not be really surprised if the policeman across the way grew wings, or if the deep sea rose and washed out the chaos of the land. I should not raise my eyebrows if the daily press became the Little Sunbeam of the Home, or if Cabinet Ministers struck for a decrease of wages. I feel no security in facts, precedent seems no protection to me. The wisdom you can find in an Encyclopedia, or in Selfridge's Information Bureau, seems to me just a transitory adaptation to quicksand circumstances.

But if the things which I know in spite of my education were false, if the eyes of the sea forgot their secret, or if the accent of the steep woods became vulgar, if the fairy adventures that happen in my heart fell flat, if the good friends my eyes have never seen failed me,—then indeed should I know emptiness, and an astonishment that would kill.

I want to introduce you to Jay, a 'bus-conductor and an idealist. She is not the heroine, but the most constantly apparent woman in this book. I cannot introduce you to a heroine because I have never met one.

She was a person who took nothing in the world for granted, but as she had only a slight connection with the world, that is not saying very much. Her answer to everything was "Why?" The fundamental facts that you and I accept from our youth upwards, like Be Good and You Will Be Happy, or Change Your Boots When You Come In Out Of The Wet, or Respect Your Elders, or Love Your Neighbour, or Never Cross Your Legs Above The Knee, did not impress Jay.

I never knew her as a baby, but I am sure she must have been born a propounder of questions, and a smiler at the answers she received. I daresay she used to ask questions—without result—long before she could talk, but I am quite sure she was not embittered by the lack of result. Nothing ever embittered Jay, not even her own pessimism. There is a finality about bitterness, and Jay was never final. Her last word was always on a questioning note. Her mind was always open, waiting for more. "Oh no," she would tell her pillow at night, "there must be a better answer than that. . ."

Perhaps it is hardly necessary to add that she had quarrelled with her Family, and run away from home. Her Family knew neither what she was doing nor where she was doing it. Families are incurably conceited, and this one supposed that, having broken away from it, Jay was going to the bad. On the contrary, she was a 'bus-conductor, but I only tell you this in confidence. I repeat the Family did not know it, and does not know it yet.

The Family sometimes said that Jay was an idealist, but it did not really think so. The Family sometimes said that she was rather mad, but it did not know how mad she was, or it would have sent her away to live in a doctor's establishment at Margate. It never realised that it had only come in contact with about one-fifth of its young relation, and that the other four-fifths were shut away from it. Shut away in a shining bubble world with only room in it for one—for One, and a shining bubble Story.

I do not know how universal an experience a Secret Story and a Secret Friend may be. Perhaps this wonder is a commonplace to you, only you are more reticent about it than Jay or I. But to me, even after twenty years' intimacy with what I can only describe as a supplementary life that I cannot describe, it still seems so very wonderful that I cannot believe I share it with every man and woman in the street.

The great advantage of a Secret Story over other stories is that you cannot put it into print. So I can only show you the initial letter, and you may if you choose look upon it as an imaginary hieroglyphic. Or you may not.

Just this, that a bubble world can contain a round and russet horizon of high woods which you can attain, and from the horizon a long view of an unending sea. You can run down across the dappled fields, you can run down into the cove and stroke the sea and hear the intimate minor singing of it. And when you feel as strong as the morning, you can shout and run against the wind, against the flying sand that never blows above your knees. And when you feel as tired as the night, you can climb slowly up the cliff path and go into the House, the House you know much better than any house your ordinary eyes have seen, and there you will find your Secret Friends. The best part about Secret Friends is that they will never weary you by knowing you. You share their House, your passing hand helps to polish the base of that wooden figure that ends the banisters, you know the childish delight of that wide short chimney in the big turret room, a chimney so wide and so short that you can stand inside the great crooked fireplace and whisper to the birds that look down from the edge of the chimney only a yard or two above you. You know how comfy those big beds are, you sit at the long clothless table in the brown dining-room. With all these things you are intimate, and yet you pass through the place as a ghost, your bubble enchantment encloses you, your Secret Friends have no knowledge of you, their story runs without you. Your unnecessary identity is tactfully ignored, and you know the heaven of being dispassionate and detached among things you love.

All these things can a bubble world contain. You have to get inside things to find out how limitless they are. And I think if you don't believe it all, it is none the less true for that, because in that case you are the sort of person who believes a thing less the truer it is.

If Jay's Family did not know she was a 'bus-conductor, and did not know she was a story-possessor, what did it know about her? It knew she disliked the smell of bananas, and that she had not taken advantage of an expensive education, and that she was Stock Size (Small Ladies'), and that she was christened Jane Elizabeth, and that she took after her father to an excessive extent, and that she was rather too apt to swallow this Socialist nonsense. As Families go, it was fairly well informed about her.

The Family was a rather promiscuous one. It had more tortuous relationships than most families have, although there were only four in it, not counting Mr. Russell.

I might as well introduce you to the Family before I settle down to the story. From careful study of the press reviews I gather that a story is considered a necessary thing in a novel, so this time I am going to try and include one.

You may, if you please, meet the Family after breakfast at Mr. Russell's house in Kensington, about three months after Jay had run away. There were four people in the room. They were Cousin Gustus, Mrs. Gustus, Kew, and Mr. Russell.

It behoves me to try and tell you very simply about Mrs. Gustus, because she prided herself on simplicity. Spelt with a capital S, it constituted her Deity; her heaven was a severe and shadowless eternity, and plain words were the flowers that grew in her Elysian fields. She had simplified her life and her looks. Even her smile was shorn of all accessories like dimples or twinkles. Her hair, which was not abundant, was the colour of corn, straight and shining. Her eyes were a cold dark grey.

Now to be simple is all very well, but turn it into an active verb and you spoil the whole idea. To simplify seems forced, and I think Mrs. Gustus struck harder on the note of simplification than that of simplicity. I should not dare to criticise her, however, and Cousin Gustus was satisfied, so criticism in any case would be intrusive. It is just possible that he occasionally wished that she would dress herself in a more human way—patronise in winter the humble Viyella stripe, for instance, or in summer the flippant sprig. But a large proportion of Mrs. Gustus's faith was founded on simple strong colours in wide expanses, introduced, as it were, one to another by judicious black. Anybody but Mrs. Gustus would have been drowned in her clothes. But she was conceived on a generous scale, she was almost gorgeous, she barely missed exaggeration. In her manner I think she did not miss it. She had therefore the gift of coping with colour. It remains for me to add that her age was five-and-forty, and that she was a novelist. The recording angel had probably noted the fact of her novelism among her virtues, but she had an imperceptible earthly public. She wrote laborious books, full of short peevish sentences, of such very pure construction that they were extremely difficult to understand. She wore spectacles with aggressive tortoise-shell rims. She said, "I am short-sighted. I am obliged to wear spectacles. Why should I try to conceal the fact? I will not have a pair of rimless ghosts haunting my face. I will wear spectacles without shame." But the real truth was that the tortoise-shell rims were more becoming to her. Mrs. Gustus was known to her husband's family as Anonyma. The origin of this habit was an old joke, and I have forgotten the point of it.

Cousin Gustus was second cousin once removed to Kew and Kew's sister Jay, and had kindly brought them up from childhood. He was now at the further end of the sixties, and embittered by many things: an unsuitable marriage, the approach of the psalmist's age-limit, incurably modern surroundings, an internal complaint, and a haunting wish to relieve the Government of the management of the War. These drawbacks were to a certain extent linked, they accounted for each other. The complaint hindered him from offering his services as Secretary of State; it made of him a slave, so he could not pretend to be a master. He cherished his slavery, for it happened to be painless, and supplied him with a certain dignity which would otherwise have been difficult to secure. During the summer the complaint hibernated, and ceased to interest either doctors or relations, which was naturally hard to bear. To these trials you may add the disgraceful behaviour of his young cousin Jay, and admit that Cousin Gustus had every excuse for encouraging pessimism of the most pronounced type.

Jay's brother Kew was twenty-five, and from this it follows that he had already drunk the surprising beverage of War. His military history included a little splinter of hate in the left shoulder, followed by a depressing period almost entirely spent in the society of medical boards, three months of light duty consisting of weary instruction of fools in an East coast town, and now an interval of leave at the end of which the battalion to which he had lately been attached hoped to go to France. In one way it was a pity he ever joined the Army, for khaki clashed badly with most of Mrs. Gustus's colour theories. But he had never noticed that: his eye and his ear and his mind were all equally slow to appreciate clashings of any kind. He was rather aloof from comparison and criticism, but not on principle. He had no principles—at least no original ones, just the ordinary stuffy old principles of decency and all that. He never turned his eyes inward, as far as the passer-by could see; he lived a breezy life outside himself. He never tried to make a fine Kew of himself; he never propounded riddles to his Creator, which is the way most of us make our reputations.

Mr. Russell, the host and adopted member of the Family, was fifty-two. He did not know Jay, having only lately been culled by Mrs. Gustus—that assiduous collector—and placed in the bosom of the Family. She had found him blossoming unloved in the wilderness of a War Work Committee. He was well informed, yet a good listener; perhaps he possessed both these virtues to excess. At any rate Mrs. Gustus had decided that he was worthy of Family friendship, and, being naturally extravagant, she conferred it upon him with both hands. Mr. Russell was married to a woman who had not properly realised the fact that she was Mrs. Russell. She spent her life in distant lands, helping the world to become better. At present she was understood to be propagating peace in the United States, and was never mentioned by or to her husband. My first impression of Mr. Russell was that he was rather fat, but I never could trace this impression to its origin. He had not exactly a double chin, but rather a chin and a half, and the rest of him followed this moderate example. His grey hair retired in a pronounced estuary over each temple, leaving a beautifully brushed peninsula between. He had no sense of humour, but hid this deformity skillfully. Hardly anybody knew that he was a poet, except presumably his dog. He often talked to his dog; he told it every speakable thought that he had. This was his only bad habit. Occasionally his dog was heard to reply in a small curious voice proceeding also from Mr. Russell.

These four people looked out at Kensington Gardens, which were rejoicing in the very babyhood of the year. The naked trees were like pillars in the mist, the grass was grey and whitened to the distance, the world had mislaid its horizon, and one's eye slid up without check between the trees to where the last word of a daylight moon whispered in the sky.

"I glory in a view that dispenses with colour," said Mrs. Gustus severely. She always spoke as though she were sure of the whole of what she intended to say. When she did hesitate, it only meant that she was seeking for the simplest word, and she would cap her pause with a monosyllable as curt as an explosion.

But glory is the right word, I think, for London in some moods. Do you know the feeling of a heart beating too high, when you see the great cliffs of London under rain or vague sunshine, or rising out of yellow air? Do you ever want, as I do, to stand with arms out against the London wind, and shout your own unmade poetry on the top of a 'bus? With this sort of grotesque glorying does London inspire me, so that I spend whole days together feeling that the essential *I* is too big for what encloses it.

Anonyma never felt like this. She often spoke the right word, but she nearly always spoke it coldly.

"This morning," said Kew, "when I looked out, I felt the futility of bed, so I made an assignation with the Hound when I met it trooping along with Russ in single file to the bathroom. Why does your Hound always accompany you there, Russ? Dogs must think us awfully irrational beasts, and yet—does that Hound really think you could elope for ever and be no more seen, with nothing on but pyjamas and a towel? I suppose he thinks 'You can't be too careful.' It makes one humble to live with a dog. I always blush when I see a dog dreaming, because I'm afraid they give us an undignified place in their dreams. Your Hound, Russ, dreams of you plunging into the Serpentine after a Canadian Goose, with your topper floating behind you, or Anonyma with her tongue hanging out, scratching at a little mousehole in Piccadilly. It is humiliating, isn't it? Anyway, before breakfast, Russ's Hound and I went and jumped over things in the Gardens. The park-keeper mistook us for young lambs."

Russell's Hound was called so by courtesy, in order to lend him a dignity which he lacked. He may have been twelve inches high at the shoulder, and he thought that he was exactly like a lion, except for a trifling difference in size. Dignity is not, of course, incompatible with small stature, but I think it was the twinkling gait of Mr. Russell's Hound that robbed him of moral weight, and prevented you from attaching great importance to his views.

"Young lambs!" exclaimed Mrs. Gustus. "Really, my good Kew, had you nothing better to do?"

"Not at that time," replied Kew. "You weren't up." And he sang to drown her sigh. Kew was the only person I ever knew who really sang to the tune of his moods. He sang Albert Hall sort of music very loudly when he was happy, and when he was extremely happy he roared so that his voice broke out of tune. When he was silent it was almost always because he was asleep, or because some other member of the Family was talking. When, by some accident, the whole Family was simultaneously silent, you could not help noticing what an oppressively still place London was. The sound of Russell's Hound sneezing in the hall was like a bomb.

But at the present moment Kew only sang a few bars of Beethoven in a small voice. He was rather sad, because of Jay. He had not realised till he came home how very thoroughly Jay had disappeared. He led the conversation to Jay. It often happened that Kew led conversations, because conversations, like the public, generally follow the loudest voice.

"Why so sudden?" asked Kew, apparently of the Round Pond, so loud was his voice. "That's what I can't make out. She used to be such a human sort, and anybody with half an ear could hear the decisions bubbling about under the lid for weeks before they boiled over."

Everybody—even Cousin Gustus—knew that he was talking of Jay. Kew said so much that he might be excused for forgetting occasionally what he had not said. Besides, he had talked of little else but Jay since he rejoined his Family two days before.

"She used to be a good girl," sighed Cousin Gustus. "So few girls are good."

Cousin Gustus is an expert pessimist. Vice, accidents, and terrible ends are his speciality. All virtue is to him an exception, and by him is immediately forgotten. In sudden deaths you cannot catch him out. If you were tossed from the horns of a bull into the jaws of a crocodile, and died of pneumonia contracted during the flight, you would not surprise Cousin Gustus. He is never at a loss for a precedent. The only way you could really astonish him would be by living a blameless life without adventure, and dying of old age in your bed.

"There were warnings," said Anonyma. "Little disagreements with Gustus."

"She wanted to bring vermin into the house," mourned Cousin Gustus.

Kew suggested: "White mice?"

"Not vermin unattended," Anonyma explained. "She wanted to adopt Brown Borough babies. She had been working desultorily in the Brown Borough since War broke out."

"That might explain the peculiar and un-Jay-like remark in her letter to you—that she would settle in no home except the Perfect Home. I hate things in capital letters."

"Why didn't she get married?" grumbled Cousin Gustus. "She was engaged for nearly three weeks to young William Morgan, a most respectable young man. So few young men—"

"She wrote to me that she couldn't keep up that engagement," said Kew. "Not even by looking upon it as War Work. She called him a 'Surface young man,' and that again seemed unlike her. She usen't to mind surfaceness. The War seems to have turned her upside down. But then, of course, the War has turned us all upside down, and in that position you generally get a rush of brains to the head. We're all feverish, that's what's the matter with us. When I was in hospital I lived for three weeks on the top of a high temperature, laughing. I want to laugh now. . . It's a damn funny world."

"I once knew a man who died of apoplexy while swearing," sniffed Cousin Gustus.

"You have been damned unlucky in your friends, Cousin Gustus," said Kew. He paused, and then added: "Besides, I hardly ever say Damn without saying Un-damn to myself afterwards. It seems a pity to waste a precious word on an inadequate cause, and I always retrieve it if I can."

"Before you came down to breakfast this morning, Kew," said Anonyma, "we had an idea."

"Only one between you in all that time?" said Kew. "I was half an hour late."

"Now, Kew, be an angel and agree with the idea. I've set my heart on it," said Mrs. Gustus.

When Mrs. Gustus talked in a womanly way like this, the change was always unmistakable. She was naturally an unnatural talker, and when she mentioned such natural things as angels, you knew she was resorting deliberately to womanly charm in order to attain her end. There was something very cold-blooded about Anonyma's womanly charm.

"Good Lord," said Kew, "I wish angels had never been invented. I never am one, only people always tell me to be one. I never get officially recognised in heaven. What is the plan?"

"There is Russell's car doing nothing," began Mrs. Gustus.

"Do you mean Christina?" interrupted Kew, shocked at such formality. "Don't call her Russell's car, it sounds so cold."

"There is Russell's Christina doing nothing," compromised Anonyma. "And petrol isn't so bad as it will be. And it's a beautiful time of year. And you are not strong yet, really. And we want Jay back."

"A procession of facts doesn't make a plan," objected Kew.

"It may lead to one, eventually," said Mrs. Gustus. "Oh, Kew, I want to go out into the country, I want to thread the pale Spring air, and hear the lambs cry. I want to brush my face against the grass, and wade in a wave of bluebells. I want to forget blood and Belgians and kiss Nature."

"Take a twenty-eight 'bus, and kiss Hampstead Heath," suggested Kew. "The Spring has got there all right."

Anonyma, behind the coffee-pot, was jotting down in a notebook the salient points in her outburst. She always placed her literary calling first. And anyway, I should be rather proud if I could talk like that about the Spring without any preparation.

"The idea originally," began Mr. Russell tentatively, "was not only formed to allow Mrs. Gustus to enjoy the Spring, but also to make you quite strong before you go back to work. And, again, not only that, but also to try and trace your sister Jay."

Will you please imagine that continual intercourse with very talkative people had made Mr. Russell an adept at vocal compression. He had now almost lost the use of his vowels, and if I wrote as he spoke, the effect would be like an advertisement for a housemaid during the shortage of wood-pulp. I spare you this.

"There are three objections to the plan," said Kew. "First, that Anonyma doesn't really want to kiss the Spring; second, that I don't really want convalescent treatment; third, that Jay doesn't really want to be traced."

When Mrs. Gustus did not know the answer to an objection she left it unanswered. This is, of course, the simplest way. She snapped her notebook.

"Oh, Kew," she said, "you promised you'd be an angel." The double row of semi-detached buttons down her breast trembled with eagerness.

"Angeller and angeller," sighed Kew, "I never committed myself so far."

"I have a clue with which to trace Jay," said Mrs. Gustus. "I had a letter from her this morning."

Kew was a satisfactory person to surprise. He is never supercilious.

"You heard from Jay!" he said, in a voice as high as his eyebrows.

The letter which Mrs. Gustus showed to Kew may be quoted here:

"This place has stood since the year twelve something, and its windows look down without even the interruption of a sill at the coming and going of the tides. It has hardly any garden, and immediately to the right and the left of it the green down brims over the top of the cliff like the froth of ale over a silver goblet. Tonight the tide is low, the sea is golden where the shallow waves break upon the sand, and ghostly green in the distance. When the tide is high, the sound and the sight of it seem to meet and make one thing. The waves press up the cliff then, and fall back on each other. Do you know the lines that are written on the face of a disappointed wave? Tonight the clouds are like castles built on the plain of the sea. There is an aeroplane at this moment— dim as a little thought—coming between two turrets of cloud. I suppose it is that I can hear, but it sounds like the distant singing of the moon. I have come here to count up my theories, to count them and pile them up like money, in heaps, according to their value. Theories are such beautiful things, there must be some use in them. Or perhaps they are like money from a distant country, and not in currency here. Yet just as sheer metal, they must have some value. . . It is wonderful that such happiness should come to me, and that it should last. I have the Sea and a Friend; there is nothing in the world I lack, and nothing that I regret. . ."

"What better clue could you want?" asked Mrs. Gustus. "We will take Christina round the sea-coast."

"Looking for silver cliffs and a golden sea," sighed Kew.

STELLA BENSON

I don't know if I have mentioned or conveyed to you that Mrs. Gustus was a determined woman. At any rate she was, and it would therefore be waste of time to describe the gradual defeat of Kew. The final stage was the despatch of Kew to call on Nana in the Brown Borough. Jay's letter had the Brown Borough postmark, so it had apparently been sent to Nana to post. Nana might be described as the Second Clue in the pursuit of Jay. She was the Family's only link with Jay. The one drawback of Nana as a clue was that she was never to be found. Mrs. Gustus had called six times, but had been repulsed on each occasion by a totally dumb front door. But then Nana never had liked Anonyma. Nana was simple herself in an amateurish, unconscious sort of way, and I expect she disliked Anonyma's professional rivalry in the matter of simplicity. But Kew was always a favourite.

The 'bus roared up the canyons of the City, and its voice accompanied Kew in his tuneful meditations. A 'bus is not really well adapted for meditation. On my feet I can stride across unseen miles musing on love, in a taxi I can think about tomorrow's dinner, but on a 'bus my thoughts will go no further than my eyes can see. So Kew, although he thought he was thinking of Jay, was really considering the words in front of him—To Stop O'Bus strike Bell at Rear.* He deduced from this that it was an Irish 'bus, and supposed that this accounted for its rather head-long behaviour. He spent some moments in imagining the MacBus, child of a sterner race, which would run gutturally without skids, and wear a different cut of bonnet.

He dismounted into a faint yellow fog diluted with a faint twilight, in the Brown Borough. The air was vague, making it not so much an impossibility to decipher the features of people approaching as a surprise to find it possible. A few rather premature bar row-flares adapted Scripture to modern conditions by hiding their light under tin substitutes for bushels, in the hope of protecting such valuables as cat's meat and bananas from aerial outrage. Kew pranced over prostrate children, and curved about the pavement to avoid artificially vivacious passers-by, who emerged from the public-houses.

Nana lived in a little alley which was like a fiord of peace running in from the shrill storm of the Brown Borough. Here little cottages shrank together, passive resisters of the twentieth century. Low crooked windows blinked through a mask of dirty creepers. Each little front

* He must have changed at the Bank into a Tilling 'bus.

garden contained a shrub, and was guarded by a low railing, although there would have been no room for a trespasser in addition to the shrub. Nana's house, at the end of the alley, looked along it to the far turmoil of the mother-street.

Kew insulted the gate, as usual, by stepping over it, and knocked at the door. He held his breath, so that he might more keenly hear the first whisperings of the floor upstairs, which would show that Nana was astir.

A gardenful of cats came and told him that his hopes were vain. Cats only exist, I think, for the chastening of man. They never come to me except to tell me the worst, and to crush me with quiet sarcasm should my optimism survive their warning.

But before the cats had finished speaking, there was a most un-Nana-like sound of bounding within, and Jay appeared. She threw herself out of the darkness of the door on to the twilit Kew.

The cats were ashamed to be seen watching this almost canine display, and went away.

"I didn't know you weren't in France," said Jay to Kew.

"I didn't know you weren't in Heaven," said Kew to Jay. "What's all this about golden seas and aeroplanes snarling around?"

"Oh, snarling. . . That's just what they do," said Jay. "Let's pretend I said that."

It seemed as if childhood turned its face to them again after a thousand years. These roaring months of War run like a sea between us and our peaceful beginnings, so that a catchword flashed across out of our past is as beautiful and as incredible as the light in a dream.

When they were little they used to bargain for expressive words. Their childhood was full of such hair-splittings as: "If you tell how we said Wank-wank to the milkman, you must let me have the old lady who had a palpitation and puffocated running after the 'bus."

They were not spontaneous people. They were born with too great a love of words, a passion for drama at the expense of truth, and a habit of overweighting common life with romance. It was perhaps good for them to have acquired such a very simple relation by marriage as Anonyma.

"About the sea," said Jay, "I'll tell you later."

"Well, tell me first why you found home so suddenly unbearable. You've stood it for eighteen years."

"I've been a child all through those eighteen years. And to a child just the fact of grown-upness is so admirable. I wonder why. But under the fierce light that beats from the eye of a woman suddenly and violently grown old, Cousin Gustus and Anonyma don't—well, Kew, do they?"

The dusk filled the room as water fills a cup, and to look up at the light of an outside lamp on the ceiling was like looking up through water at the surface. Jay wore a dress of the same colour of the dusk, and her round face, faint as a bubble, seemed to float on its background unsupported.

"Didn't you think about adopting a baby?" suggested Kew. "That evidently put Cousin Gustus's back up."

"I didn't put Cousin Gustus's back up so high as he put mine," answered Jay. "Oh, Kew, what are the old that they should check us? What's the use of this war of one generation against another? Old people and young people reach a deadlock that's as bad as marriage without the possibility of divorce. Isn't all forced fidelity wrong?"

"What did you do, tell me, and what are you going to do?"

"Oh well, I felt something like frost in the air, and I couldn't define it. Really, it was work waiting to be done. Not work for the poor, but work with the poor. At home I talked about work, and Anonyma wrote about it, and Cousin Gustus shuddered at it. You were doing it all right, but where was I? Three days a week with soldiers' wives. My brow never sweated a drop. I thought there must be something better than a bird's-eye view of work. So I took a job at a bolster place. . . Oh well, it doesn't matter now. I earned ten shillings a week, and paid half-a-crown for a little basement back. On Saturdays I got my Sunday clothes out of pawn, and came to tea with Nana. Do you remember the scones and the Welsh Rarebit that Nana used to make? I believe those things were worth the terror of the pawnshop. Oh, Kew, those pawnshops! Those little secret stalls that put shame into you where none was before. The pawn man—why is it that when you're already frightened is the moment that men choose to frighten you? Because weakness is the worst crime. That I have proved. My work was putting fluff into bolsters. There was a big bright grocers' calendar—the Death of Nelson—and if I could see it through the fog of fluff I felt that was a lucky day. I had to eat my lunch there, raspberry jam sandwiches—not fruit jam, you know, but raspberry flavour. It wasn't nice, and it used to get fluffy in that air. The others sat round and munched and picked their teeth and read Jew newspapers. Have you ever noticed that whichever way up you look at a Jew newspaper, you always feel as if you could read it better if you were standing on your head? My governor was a Jew too. He wasn't bad, but he looked wet, and his hair was a horror to me. His voice was tired of dealing with fluff—though he didn't deal with it so intimately as we did—and it only allowed him to whisper. The forewoman was always cross, but always as if she would rather not be so, as if she were being cross for a bet, and as if some one were watching her to see she was not kind by mistake. She looked terribly ill, because she had worked there for three months, which was a record. I stood it five weeks, and then I had a hemorrhage—only from the throat, the doctor said. I wanted to go to bed, but you can't, because the panel doctors in these parts will not come to you. My doctor was half an enormous mile away, and it seemed he only existed between seven and nine in the evenings. So I stayed up, so as not to get too weak to walk. I went and asked the governor for my stamps. I had only five stamps due to me, only five valuable threepences had been stopped out of my wages. But I had a silly conviction at that time that the Insurance Act was invented to help working people. What an absurd idea of mine! I went to the Jew for my card. He said mine was a hard case, but I was not entitled to a card; nobody under thirty, he said, was allowed by law to have a card. So I said it was only fair to tell him I was going to the Factory and Insurance Inspectors about him. I told him lots of things, and I was so angry that I cried. He was very angry too, and made me feel sick by splashing his wet hair about. He said it was unfair for ladies to interfere in things they knew nothing about. I said I interfered because I knew nothing about it, but that now I knew. I said that ladies and women had exactly the same kind of inside, and it was a kind that never thrived on fluff instead of food. I told him how I spent my ten shillings. He couldn't interrupt really, because he had no voice. Then I fainted, and a friend I have there, called Mrs. Love, came in. She had been listening at the door. She was very good to me.

"Then, when I was well again, I found another job, but I shan't tell you what it is. As for the Inspectors, I complained, but—what's the use? So long as you must put fluff of that pernicious kind into bolsters, just so long will you kill the strength and the beauty of women. It looked so like a deadlock that it frightened me, and now in this wonderful life I lead, my Friend won't let me think of it. A deadlock is a dreadful accident, isn't it? because in theory it doesn't exist. I am working for a new end now. Isn't it splendid that there is really no Place Called Stop? There is always an end beyond the end, always something to love and

STELLA BENSON

look forward to. Life is a luxury, isn't it? there's no use in it—but how delightful!"

"You haven't told me about the sea yet," said Kew.

"Because I don't think you'd believe me. We were always liars, weren't we? That's because we're romantic, or if it's not romance, the symptoms of the disease are very like. Why can't we get rid of it all as Anonyma does? She has no gift except the gift of being able to get rid of superfluous romance. She takes that great ease impersonally, her pose is, 'It's a gift from Heaven, and an infernal bore.' But I never get nearer to joy than I do in this Secret World of mine, and with my Secret Friend."

"But what is it? What is he like?"

"I should be guilty of the murder of a secret if I told you. He isn't particularly romantic. I have seen him in a poor light; I have watched him in a most undignified temper; I have known him when he wanted a shave. I don't exist in this World of mine. I am just a column of thin air, watching with my soul."

"Then you're really telling lies to Anonyma when you write about it all? I'm not reproaching you of course, I only want to get my mind clear."

"I suppose they're lies," assented Jay ruefully, "though it seems sacrilege to say so, for I know these things better than I know myself. But Truth—or Untruth, what's the use of words like that when miracles are in question?"

"Oh, damn this What's the Use Trick," said Kew. "I suppose you picked that up in this private Heaven of yours. The whole thing's absolutely—My dear little Jay, am I offending you?"

"Yes," said Jay.

Kew sighed.

Chloris sighed too. Chloris had played the thankless part of third in this interview. She was Jay's friend, a terrier with a black eye. She shared Jay's burning desire to be of use, and, like most embryo reformers, she had a poor taste in dress. She wore her tail at an aimless angle, without chic; her markings were all lopsided. But her soul was ardent, and her life was always directed by some rather inscrutable theory or other. As a puppy she had been an inspired optimist, with legs like strips of elastic clumsily attached to a winged spirit. Later she had adopted a vigorous anarchist policy, and had inaugurated what was probably known in her set as the "Bite at Sight Campaign." Cured of this, she had become a gentle Socialist, and embraced the belief that all property—especially edible property—should be shared. Appetites, she argued, were meant to be appeased, and the preservation of game—or anything else—in the larder was an offence against the community. Now, at the age of five or so, she affected cynicism, pretended temporarily that life had left a bitter taste in her mouth, and sighed frequently.

"Kew," said Jay presently, "will you promise not to tell the Family you saw me? I don't want it to know about me. After all, theories are driving me, and theories don't concern that Family of ours. What's the use of a Family? (I'm saying this just to exasperate you.) A Family's just a little knot of not necessarily congenial people, with Fate rubbing their heads together so as to strike sparks of love. Love—what's the use of Love? I'd like to catch that Love and box his ears, making such a fool of the world. What's the use?"

"God knows," said Kew. "Cheer up, my friend, I promise I won't tell the Family I've seen you, or anything about you." At the same moment he remembered the motor tour.

"Promise faithfully?"

"Faithfully."

"It's a lovely word faithful, isn't it?" she said, wriggling in her chair. "Yours faithfully is a most beautiful ending to a letter. Why is it that faith with a little F is such a perfect thing, and yet Faith, grown-up Faith in Church, is so tiring?"

"Perhaps one is overworked and the other isn't," suggested Kew.

As he went out into the darkness the noise of London sprang into his ears, and the remote brown room where he had left Jay seemed to become divided from him by great distances. The town was like a garden, and he, an insect, pressed through its undergrowth. The rare lamps and the stars flowered above him.

My yesterday has gone, has gone, and left me tired;
And now tomorrow comes and beats upon the door;
So I have built today, the day that I desired,
Lest joy come not again, lest peace return no more,
Lest comfort come no more.

So I have built today, a proud and perfect day,
And I have built the towers of cliffs upon the sands.
The foxgloves and the gorse I planted on my way.
The thyme, the velvet thyme, grew up beneath my hands,
Grew pink beneath my hands.

So I have built today, more precious than a dream;
And I have painted peace upon the sky above;
And I have made immense and misty seas that seem
More kind to me than life, more fair to me than love,
More beautiful than love.

And I have built a House, a House upon the brink
Of high and twisted cliffs,—the sea's low singing fills it.
And there my Secret Friend abides, and there I think
I'll hide my heart away before tomorrow kills it,
A cold tomorrow kills it.

Yes, I have built today, a wall against tomorrow,
So let tomorrow knock, I shall not be afraid,
For none shall give me death, and none shall give me sorrow,
And none shall spoil this darling day that I have made.
No storm shall stir my sea. No night but mine shall shade
This day that I have made.

W e will start on our quest tomorrow," said Anonyma. "Today I must work."

Nobody in Anonyma's circle was ever allowed to forget that she spent four hours a week in the service of her country. You would never guess how much insight into the souls of the poor, four hours a week can give to a person like Anonyma. She had written two books about the Brown Borough since the outbreak of War. The provincial Press had been much impressed by their vivid picture of slum realities. Anonyma's poor were always yearning, yearning to be understood and loved by a ministering upper class, yearning for light, for art, for self-expression, for novels by high-souled ladies. The atmosphere of Anonyma's fiction was thick with yearning.

Anonyma always came home from her Work with what she called "word-vignettes" in her notebook. She gave her Family the benefit of these during the rest of the week, besides fitting them into her books. So that although Cousin Gustus always conscientiously bought a dozen copies of each novel as it came out, he really wasted his money, for he was obliged to know all his wife's copy by heart before it got into print. By speaking each thought as well as writing it, Anonyma rather unfairly won a reputation twice over with the same material.

Anonyma produced a vignette now, in order to show how necessary it was that she should hurry to her yearning flock.

"I came into the room of one of my sailors' wives last week, and I found her with a baby sobbing on her breast, and an empty hearth at her feet. I thought of the eternal tragedy of womanhood. I said, 'Will my love help, my dear?'"

There was a pause, and Cousin Gustus sighed.

"What did she say?" asked Kew, without expecting an answer from the artist. After all, a word-vignette is not intended to have a sequel. It is supposed to fall complete with a little splash into your silent understanding. I must say Kew was rather tiresome in refusing to be content with the splash.

"So few women really understand how to stop a child crying," said Cousin Gustus, speaking from bitter and universal experience.

"That's the point," said Kew. "The child had probably swallowed a pin."

It generally breaks my heart to hear a story spoilt, but with Anonyma's word-vignettes I did not mind, because they were told as true, and yet they did not ring true. I must tell you that Anonyma had married into a family of accomplished white liars, and to them the ring of truth was as unmistakable as the dinner-bell. Few people could lie successfully to Kew or Jay, they knew that art from the inside. White lies are easily justified, but almost any lie can be whitewashed. Apart from the mutual attitude of Kew and Jay, who possessed something between them that might be called good faith, there was hardly any trust included in that family relationship. Cousin Gustus distrusted youth. He thought young people were always either lying to him or laughing at him, and indeed they often were. Only not so often as he thought. He was no prop on which to repose confidence, and it was very easy both to tell him lies and not to tell him facts.

Mrs. Gustus had no gift of intimacy. She was reserved about everything except herself, or what she believed to be herself. The self that she shared so generously with others was, however, not founded on fact, but modelled on the heroine of all her books. She killed her heroine whenever possible—I think she only once married her,—yet still the creature remained immortal in Mrs. Gustus's public personality. She concealed or transformed everything that did not seem artistic. Her notebook was a tangle of self-deceptions. The rest of the Family knew this. They never pretended to believe her.

Kew and Jay were skilled romancers, fact was clay in their hands. Nobody had ever taught them such a dull lesson as exact truthfulness. If they built the bare bones of their structures fairly accurately, they placed the whole in an artificial light, altering in some effective way the spirit of the facts. Education had impressed the importance of technical truthfulness on Kew. But he was a quick talker, and in order to keep him in line with his tongue, nature had made him quick of wit, quick in argument, and unconsciously quick in making and seeing loopholes for escape.

He was at present perfectly comfortable in his anomalous position regarding a search round the sea-coast for a Jay he knew to be in the Brown Borough.

"If I am going to work, I must go," said Anonyma. "Russ and I will go together as far as the Underground."

She looked at herself in the glass. The scarlet bird in her hat had an arresting expression. As she was putting on her gloves she said, "I'm sorry, Kew, about your disappointment, not finding Nana at home last night. But I told you so."

She had no fear of this much-shunned phrase.

　　　　　　　　　　　　　　　　STELLA BENSON

"Never mind," said Kew mildly. "We'll put Christina on the track tomorrow."

Mr. Russell said a polite Good-bye to his Hound, and accompanied his friend Anonyma to the Underground. That was a fateful little journey for him.

As he turned from Anonyma's side at the bookstall, he noticed a 'bus positively beckoning to him. It had a lady conductor, and she was poised expectantly, one hand on the bell and the other beckoning to Mr. Russell. His nature was docile, and the 'bus was bound for Chancery Lane, his destination. He mounted the 'bus.

I need hardly tell you that a 'bus that makes deliberate advances to the public is the rarest sight in London. The self-respecting 'bus looks upon the public as dust beneath its tyres. Even a Brigadier-General with red tabs, on his way to Whitehall, looks pathetically humble waggling his cane at a 'bus. All 'bus-drivers have a kingly look; it comes from their proud position. The rest of the world is only worthy to communicate with that noble race by means of nods and becks and wreathed smiles.

"Chancery Lane, please," said Mr. Russell. "But why did you stop specially for me?"

"I thought your wife hailed me, sir," lied the 'bus-conductor.

Any allusion to his wife mildly annoyed Mr. Russell. "Not my wife," he said. "Merely a friend."

"Oh, I *beg* your pardon, sir," said the 'bus-conductor, and underlined the "beg" with the ting of her ticket-puncher. She was rather a darling 'bus-conductor, because she was also Jay. She had a short, though not a fat face, soft eyes, and very soft hair cut short to just below the lobes of her ears.

A gentleman with dingy but elaborate boot-uppers hailed and mounted the 'bus. "Shufftesbury Uvvenue?" he asked. He said it that way, of course, because he was a Shakespearian actor. The 'bus-conductor gave him his ticket, and then took her stand upon her platform, more or less unaware that Mr. Russell and the actor, both next to the door and opposite to each other, were looking at her with a pleased look.

Mr. Russell thought for some time, and then he said, "'T's a b'tiful day."

"That's what it is," replied the 'bus-conductor. "I wonder if it's wrong to enjoy being a 'bus-conductor?"

"I shouldn't think so," said Mr. Russell cautiously. "Why?"

The 'bus-conductor waved her hand towards a State hint that shouted in letters six foot high from an opposite wall: "Don't Use A Motor Car For Pleasure." Mr. Russell read it very carefully and said nothing.

"This is a motor car," observed the 'bus-conductor, glancing at her inaccessible chauffeur. "And as for pleasure. . ."

The high houses rose out of the earth like Alps, and the roar in the morning was like large music. She knew she had been an Olympian in a recent life, because she found herself familiar with greater and more gorgeous speed than any 'bus attains, and with the divine discords that high mountains and high cities sing.

"I hope it's not wrong, because I'm going on a motor tour tomorrow," said Mr. Russell. "On business of a sort, and yet also on pleasure. On a search, as a matter of fact."

"Oh, any search is pleasure," said the bus-conductor. "Especially if it's an abstract search."

"'Tisn't," said Mr. Russell. "'T's a search for a person."

The 'bus-conductor looked at the sky. "And are Anonyma and Kew going too?" she thought. You must bear in mind that she had deliberately plucked him from the side of Anonyma.

"Perhaps any pleasure is wrong in these days," she said.

"Come, come," said the actor. "Whut's wrung with these days? A German ship sunk yesterday. Thut's pleasurable enough."

The 'bus-conductor turned a cold eye upon him.

"I can cheer, but not laugh over such news as that," she said pompously. "Doesn't even a German find the sea bitter to drown in? An English woman or a German butcher, isn't it all the same when it comes to a Me, with a throat full of water? Hasn't a German got a Me?"

The actor looked at his boot-uppers. Mr. Russell thought. Shufftesbury Uvvenue arrived soon, and the actor alighted with some relief.

When the 'bus started again, the bus-conductor said, "Don't you think the only way you can get pleasure out of it all is by treating life as a bead upon a string?"

"That's a sufficient way, surely," said Mr. Russell. "If you can truly reach it."

In the Strand he asked, "May I come in this 'bus again?"

"This is a public 'bus," observed the 'bus-conductor.

"This is Monday," said Mr. Russell. "May I gather that during this week your 'bus will be passing Kensington Church at half-past eleven every morning?"

The 'bus-conductor did not answer. She went to the top of the 'bus to say, "Fezz plizz."

Mr. Russell thought so furiously that he was only roused by the sound of St. Paul's striking apparently several dozen in his immediate vicinity.

"This is Ludgate Hill. I only paid you as far as Chancery Lane. I owe you another halfpenny," said Mr. Russell.

"A penny," said the 'bus-conductor.

As he disappeared she thought, "There is something remarkable about that man. I wish I hadn't been so prosy. I wonder where and why Anonyma picked him up."

When Mr. Russell came home that evening, he said, "I met—"

"Isn't it wonderful—the people and the things one meets?" said Mrs. Gustus. "I met today a child with nothing but one garment on, rolling like a sparrow in the dust. The one garment, I thought, was the only drawback in the scene. Why can't we get back to simplicity?"

Mr. Russell, on second thoughts, was glad he had been interrupted. He did not feel discouraged, only he decided not to try again. His Hound jumped on to his knee and put a paw into his hand.

"I also persuaded a woman to give up drink," continued Mrs. Gustus. "I put it to her on the ground of simplicity. She was in bed, having been drunk the night before, and I sat on her bed with my hand on hers. I said, 'Dear fellow-woman, there are no essentials in life but bread and water and love. Everything else is a sort of skin-disease which has appeared on the surface of Nature, a disease which we call civilization.' She cried bitterly, and I gathered that she was lacking in all three essentials. I went and bought her four loaves of bread, on condition she would promise never to touch intoxicants again. I said I would not go away until she promised. She promised. I left her still crying."

Cousin Gustus sighed. He never went about himself, and only saw the world through his wife's eyes. This did not tend to cure his pessimism.

"It is wonderful how one can reach the bed-rock of life in two hours among the poor and simple," said Mrs. Gustus. "By the way, I only put in two hours today, because I think I can do better work in two hours twice a week than in four hours once. So I shall come up for the afternoon one day this week from wherever we are by then, and leave you three men prostrate on some shore, with your ears to Nature, like a child's ear to a shell."

She groped for her notebook.

"I must come up now and then too," said Mr. Russell, and poked his Hound secretly in the ribs.

I CAN'T TELL YOU WHAT countless miles away his 'bus-conductor was by now. A certain fraction of her, to be sure, was sitting in the dark room at Number Eighteen Mabel Place, Brown Borough, with fierce hands pinching the table-cloth, and a hot forehead on the table. All day long the thirst for a secret journey had been in her throat. All day long the elaborate tangle of London had made difficult her way, but she had kicked aside the snare now, and her free feet were on the step of the House by the Sea.

No voices met her at the door, the hall was empty. The firelight pencilled in gold the edges of the wooden figure that presided over the stairs. I think I told you about that figure. I never knew whose it was—a saint's I think, but her virtuous expression was marred by her broken nose, and the finger with which she had once pointed to Heaven was also broken. Her figure was rather stiff, and so were her draperies, which fell in straight folds to her blocklike feet. Her right hand was raised high, and her left was held alertly away from her side and had unseparated fingers. She had seen a great procession of generations pass her pedestal, but she never saw Jay. Of course not, for Jay was not there. Only a column of thin watching air haunted the House.

There are many ghosts that haunt the House by the Sea. Jay is, of course, one of them, and for this reason she knows more about ghosts than any one I know. Fragments of untold stories are familiar to her. She knows how you may hear in the dark a movement by your bed, and fling out your hand and feel it grasped, and then feel the grasp slide up from your hand to your shoulder, from your shoulder to your throat, from your throat to your heart. She knows how you may go between trees in the moonlight to meet your friend, and find suddenly that some one is keeping pace with you, and how you, mistaking this companion for your friend, may say some silly greeting that only your friend understands. And how your heart drops as you hear the first breath of the reply. She knows how, walking in the mid-day streets of London, you may cross the path of some Great One who had a prior right by many thousand years to walk beside the Thames. These are the ghost stories that never get told. Few people can read them between the lines of press accounts of inquests, or in the dignified announcements of the failure of hearts, on the front page of the *Morning Post*. But Jay knows, because of her intimacy with the House by the Sea. There she meets her fellow-ghosts.

The House, as I told you, has hardly any garden; having the sea, it doesn't need one. But there is a little formal place about twenty paces across, set, as it were, in the heart of the House. A small prim square, bounded on the north, south and east by the House itself, and on the west by the cliff and the sea. There is a stone balustrade to divide the garden from space. In the middle of the square is a stone basin with becalmed water-lilies and of course goldfish. Round the basin the orderly ranks of little clipped box hedges manoeuvre. The untamed elements in the garden are the climbing things, they sing in gold and yellow and orange and red from the walls. The only official way into the garden is a door from the House, a bald door without eyebrows, so to speak, like all the doors and windows in the House. But there is an unofficial way into the garden, and Jay found her Secret Friend there. This is the short cut to the sea. In other words, it is a wriggly ladder, one end of which you attach to a hook in the wall, and the other you throw over the balustrade down the cliff to the sea. It is a long way to walk round the House and along the cliff and down to the sea by the path. And just as the house-agents always want to be one minute and a half from the church and the post-office, so we in the Secret House cannot afford to be more than a minute and a half from the sea.

The Secret Friend was there, and he was gazing so earnestly down the cliff that his hair was hanging forward most unbeautifully, and he was rather red in the face. He was looking at a little boat which was on its way towards the foot of the wriggly ladder. A schooner with the low sun climbing down her rigging breathed on the breathing sea not far away. The tide was high.

The oars of the little boat suddenly wavered and were paralysed. One of the rowers made a quick movement with his hand.

"It's the Law," said the Secret Friend, and he tried spasmodically to extinguish the sun with his hand. "It's the Law. The man with the tall and dewy brow."

The Law, in a fat officious-looking boat, came sneaking round the near point of the cliff. The air was so still, and the sea so calm, that you could hear the sides of the boat grate against the cliff. And the air was so clear that you could see the tall and dewy brow of the Law, as he stood up and discovered the wriggly ladder.

"To have a face like that," said the Secret Friend, "is to challenge fate. It makes me sick."

"What is this?" asked the Law, although there seemed little doubt that the thing was a wriggly ladder. No one answered; so the Law rowed to the foot of the thing in question. The Secret Friend jerked it up about six feet, and secured it so.

The Law cleared its throat, and looked nervously at the schooner, and at the sun, and at the other boat, and at the Secret Friend. The Law likes to be argued with. Take away words and where is the Law? Silence always annoys it.

Yet there was no silence in the Secret World. I remember how the roses sang, and how the sea mourned over the confusion of its gentle dreams. The knocking of the slow sea upon the cliff seemed like the ticking of the great clock that is our world. It was a night when every horizon had heaven calling from the other side.

The Story went on. . .

It was Chloris who brought Jay back to Number Eighteen Mabel Place, Brown Borough. Chloris gave an unromantic snort and sat with unnecessary clumsiness upon Jay's toe. So Jay returned, falling suddenly out of the music of the sea into the band-of-hopeful music of distant Boy Scouts on the march.

Number Eighteen Mabel Place is not, as a rule, a hopeful place to return to. Jay and I know quite well what Satan felt like when he was expelled from Heaven.

So Jay, whose refuge from most ills was talk, went to see a friend. She had many friends in the Brown Borough, and most of them were what Mrs. Gustus would call "undeserving." Mrs. Gustus has a very high mind; she and the C.O.S. are dreadfully grown-up institutions, I think; they forget what it feels like to have a good rampageous kick against the pricks. Nearly everybody in the Brown Borough enjoys a kick once a week (on pay-day)—and some of us go on kicking all our lives. At any rate, the Brown Borough is peopled with babies young and old, and high minds and grown-up institutions are apt to look over heads. Jay had a low mind and walked about on the Brown Borough level.

"I have got neuralgia," said Jay to Chloris, "my hat feels too tight. My head feels like *tête de veau farcie*. I shall go and talk to Mrs. 'Ero Edwards."

And so she did, and found that Mrs. 'Ero Edwards had been wanting to see her to tell her that the war would be over in June, and that the Edwards's nephew knew on the best authority that the Kaser couldn't get no kipper to his breakfast any more because Preserdink Wilson was a-holding of them up upon the high seas, and that Jimmy Wragge was "wanted" for "helping himself," and that young Dusty Morgan, the lodger, had gone for a soldier, and his wife had taken his job as driver of a van.

"There's only two jobs now," said Mrs. 'Ero Edwards, "wot you never see a woman doin', and one's a burglar, an' the other's a scarecrow."

Jay said, "The lady burglars would be so clever they'd never get into the papers, and the lady scarecrows would be so attractive that they'd fascinate the birds."

And then Mrs. 'Ero Edwards considered what she would say to an 'Un if she had him here, and Jay was called upon to provide 'Unnish replies in the 'Unnish lingo. Her German was so patriotically rusty that she could think of no better retorts than "Nicht hinauslehnen," or "Bitte nicht zu rauchen," or "Heisses Wasser, bitte," or "Wacht am Rhein," or "Streng verboten." Yet the dramatic effect of the interview was very good indeed, and Mrs. 'Ero Edwards's arguments were unanswerable in any tongue.

And then they thought they would make a surprise for young Mrs. Dusty Morgan, the lodger, against she come back from work, because she was that down'earted. So they went and bought some ribbon to tie up the curtains, and some flowers for the table, and put the chairs in happy and new attitudes of expectancy, and cleaned the windows, putting a piece of white paper on the broken pane instead of the rag, which was rather weary of its job. And then Mrs. 'Ero Edwards confided to Jay that young Mrs. Dusty wanted very much to find the picture of a real tip-top soldier, so that she might look at it and remember how this business was going to make a man of young Dusty. And Jay went all the way to the City and could find no picture of a tip-top soldier, and then she came back to the Brown Borough, and because of the intervention of Providence, found Albrecht Dürer's "St. George" second-hand in a Jew-shop. And they hung it up over the mantelpiece, and decided that it was rather like Dusty, if it wasn't for the uniform.

And the general effect was so superb that Jay nearly spoilt it all by jumping a hole in the floor, so as to jog Time's elbow and bring Mrs. Dusty home quickly to see it all. It was a very delicate floor. Jay always jumped when she was impatient. She did everything with double fervour, and where you or I would have stamped one foot, she stamped two at once.

Mrs. Dusty Morgan came back a little bit drunk. When she saw the Saint over the mantelpiece she cried, and blasted the war that made it necessary to wear them. . . respirators all over (the Saint is in armour),— and when she saw the flowers, she laughed, and said it seemed like Nothing-on-Earth to have Dusty away.

Oh, bend your eyes, nor send your glance about.
Oh, watch your feet, nor stray beyond the kerb.
Oh, bind your heart lest it find secrets out.
For thus no punishment
Of magic shall disturb
Your very great content.

Oh, shut your lips to words that are forbidden.
Oh, throw away your sword, nor think to fight.
Seek not the best, the best is better hidden.
Thus need you have no fear,
No terrible delight
Shall cross your path, my dear.

Call no man foe, but never love a stranger.
Build up no plan, nor any star pursue.
Go forth with crowds; in loneliness is danger.
Thus nothing Fate can send,
And nothing Fate can do
Shall pierce your peace, my friend.

C hristina the motor car started next morning. She set her tyres on the road to the Secret World. For all the clues that Jay provided pointed to that region.

"Here is another letter from Jay," said Mrs. Gustus as they started, bristling with clues. Odd, under the circumstances, that she writes to me so often and so freely. I will read you some of it, but not all, until I have thought my suspicions over. She writes:

". . . A collision with the Law tonight, under a great sunset. It would have been rather silly by common daylight, but under a yellow sky with stars in it, I think nothing can live but romance. The tide was coming up, and the Law—a man with a tall and dewy brow—rowed up to the foot of our little ladder that leads to the sea. . . You know those round stone balls that sit on the balustrades of formal gardens such as this. . . we only meant to frighten the Law, a splash was all that we intended, but the sun was in my Friend's eyes as he dropped the ball. It struck the bow of the boat, which went under like a frightened porpoise. There were two men in it, besides the Law itself, and they all came up spitting and spouting, and stood up to their necks in water. Oaths bubbled up to us. The boat came up badly perforated, and I expect we shall get into trouble. It was funny, but the War has rather pacified us peace-time belligerents, and made people like me unused to collisions with authority. I felt very nervous, but it was all right because. . ."

"I will read you no more, but in that much there should be several clues. We must keep the western sun in our eyes to begin with."

"We must look out for a householder of irregular—not to say murderous—habits," said Cousin Gustus. "Juggling with stone balls is a trick that is frequently fatal. Nobody but Jay would encourage it."

"We must comb out all western seaside resorts for local police with tall and dewy brows," said Kew.

But Mr. Russell, who preferred not to speak and drive Christina at the same time, drew up to the kerb, and removed his gloves, preparatory to saying something of importance.

Mr. Russell was at his best in a car, or, to put it another way, he was at his worst everywhere else. When he and Christina went out together they were only one entity. They were a centaur on wheels; Mr. Russell could feel the rushing of the road beneath his tyres, and I think if you had stuck a pin into the back seat, Mr. Russell would have known it. You could feel now the puzzled growl of Christina's engines as Mr. Russell pondered.

"But I remember. . ." said Mr. Russell. "Now, did I see it in the paper. . . ? I remember. . . Half a minute, it is coming back."

"Here's today's paper," said Kew, who was getting a little confused. You will feel the same when you set out to follow the western sun in search of something you know you have left behind you.

Mr. Russell and Christina lingered beside the kerb for quite a minute, and then shrugged their shoulders and started again.

So the Family set their faces towards the Secret World, with Mr. Russell as their guide, and the morning sun behind them.

London is a friend whom I can leave knowing without doubt that she will be the same to me when I return, tomorrow or forty years hence, and that, if I do not return, she will sing the same song to inheritors of my happy lot in future generations. Always, whether sleeping or waking, I shall know that in Spring the sun rides over the silver streets of Kensington, and that in the Gardens the shorn sheep find very green pasture. Always the plaited threads of traffic will wind about the reel of London; always as you go up Regent Street from Pall Mall and look back, Westminster will rise with you like a dim sun over the horizon of Whitehall. That dive down Fleet Street and up to the black and white cliffs of St. Paul's will for ever bring to mind some rumour of romance. There is always a romance that we leave behind in London, and always London enlocks that flower for us, and keeps it fresh, so that when we come back we have our romance again.

Mr. Russell was a lover of London, and that is why he liked his new-found 'bus-conductor. He was an uncalculating sort of man, and he only thought that he had found a flower in London, a very London flower, and he hoped that London would show it to him again. He had no instinct either for the past or the future. He never looked back over the road he had trod, unless he was obliged to, and he never tried to look forward to the end of the road he was treading.

Mrs. Gustus, with an iron expression about her chin, kept time to the beat of Christina's engine with the throbbing of disagreeable thoughts. There was one thing very plain to her in the matter of Jay— that Jay was living a life that in a novel is called free, but in a Family— well—you know what. . . Mrs. Gustus knew all about these Friends with capital F's, Friends with hair flopping over their foreheads, Friends who might drop stone balls on the Law and still retain their capital F's. She had, in fact, written about them with much daring and freedom. But one's young relations may never share the privileges of one's heroines. Sympathy with such goings on must be confined to the printed page.

"I will keep these things from the others," thought Mrs. Gustus. "They have no suspicions, and if we can find Jay I may be able to save her reputation yet."

Really she was thinking as much of her own good name as of Jay's. For there was a most irritating similarity between Jay's present apparent practices and Mrs. Gustus's own much-expressed theories. The beauty of a free life of simplicity had filled pages of Anonyma's notebooks, and also, to the annoyance of Cousin Gustus, had overflowed into her conversation. Cousin Gustus's memory had been constantly busy extracting from the past moral tales concerning the disasters attendant on excessive simplicity in human relationships. For a time it had seemed as if Cousin Gustus's lot had been cast entirely with the matrimonially unorthodox. And now Mrs. Gustus, for one impatient minute, wished that the children would pay more attention to their elderly and experienced guardian. It was too much to ask her—a professional theory-maker—to adapt her theories to the young and literal. That was the worst of Jay, she was so literal, so unimaginative, so lacking in the simple unpractical quality of poetry. However, not a word to the others. Jay's reputation and Anonyma's dignity might yet be saved.

"I don't know where we are going," said Anonyma presently. "I have no bump of locality."

She always spoke proudly of her failings, as though there were a rapt press interviewer at her elbow, anxious to make a word-vignette about her.

Mr. Russell was thinking, and Kew was singing, so between them they forgot to shape the course of Christina due west. When they got outside London, they found themselves going south.

To go out of London was like going out of doors. The beauty of London is a dim beauty, and while you are in the middle of it you forget what it is like to see things clearly. In London every hour is a hill of adventure, and in the country every hour is a dimple in a quiet expanse of time.

The Family went out over the hills of Surrey, and between roadside trees they saw the crowned heads of the seaward downs. The horizon sank lower around them, the fields and woods circled and squared the ribs of the land.

Before sunset they had reached the little town that guards the gate in the wall of the Sussex downs. They were welcomed by a thunderstorm, and by passionate rain that drove them to the inn. Christina, torn between her pride of soul and her pride of paint, was obliged to edge herself into a shed which was already occupied by two cows and a red and blue waggon.

When the pursuers of Jay set their feet on the uneven floor of the inn, they recognised the place immediately as ideal. Its windows squinted, its floor made you feel as though you were drunk, its banisters reeled, its flights of stairs looked frequently round in an angular way at their own beginnings.

"How Arcadian!" said Mrs. Gustus, as she splashed her signature into the visitor's book. "One could be content to vegetate for ever here. Isn't it pathetic how one spends one's life collecting heart's desires, until one suddenly discovers that in having nothing and in desiring nothing lies happiness."

But when they had been shown their sitting-room, and had ordered their supper—lamb and early peas and gooseberry tart with *tons* of cream—Mrs. Gustus saw the Ring, that great green breast of the country, against the broken evening sky, and said, "Now I see heights, and I shall never be happy or hungry till I have climbed them. The Lord made me so that I am never content until I am as near the sky as possible. Silly, no doubt. But what a sky! Blood-red and pale pink, what a unique chord of colour."

"Same chord as the livery of the Bank or England," said Kew, who was hungry, and had an aching shoulder. He hated beauty talked, just as he hated poetry forced into print apropos of nothing. Even to hear the Psalms read aloud used to make him blush, before his honest orthodoxy hardened him.

Mrs. Gustus asked the lamb and gooseberry tart to delay their coming; she placed Cousin Gustus in an arm-chair, first wrapping him up because he felt cold, and then unwrapping him again because he felt hot; she kissed him good-bye.

"We shan't be more than an hour," she said. When Mrs. Gustus said an hour, she meant two. If she had meant an hour, she would have said twenty minutes. "You must watch for us to appear on the highest point of the Ring."

"Don't watch, but pray," murmured Kew. "There's that thunderstorm just working up to another display."

And so it was, but when they reached the ridge of down that led to the Ring, they were glad they had come. They were half-drowned, and half-blinded, and half-deafened, but there is a reward to every effort. There was an enormous sky, and the sunlight spilled between the clouds to fall in pools upon the world. There was a chord made by many larks in the sky; the valleys held joy as a cup holds water. From the down the chalk-pits took great bites; the crinolined trees curtseyed down the slopes. The happy-coloured sea cut the world in half; the sight of a distant town at the corner of the river and the coast made one laugh for pleasure. There was a boat with sunlit sails creeping across the sea. I never see a boat on an utterly lonely sea without thinking of the secret stories that it carries, of the sun moving round that private world, of the shadows upon the deck that I cannot see, of the song of passing seas that I cannot hear, of the night coming across a great horizon to devour it when I shall have forgotten it. Further off and more suggestive than a star, it seems to me.

A gust of sunlight struck the watchers, and passed: they each ran a few steps towards the sight that pleased them most. And then they stood so long that Mr. Russell's Hound had time to make himself acquainted with every smell within twenty yards. He turned over a snail that sat—round and striped like a peppermint bull's-eye—on the short grass, he patted a little beetle that pushed its way across a world of disproportionate size, and then, by peevishly pulling the end of his whip which hung from Mr. Russell's pensive hand, he suggested that the pursuit should continue. So they walked to the crest of wood that stands at the top of the Ring, a compressed tabloid forest, fifty yards from side to side, as round as a florin piece.

The slopes rushed away from every side of it. There was a dark secret beneath those trees, there was a hint of very ancient love and still more ancient hatred. You could feel things beyond understanding, you left fact outside under the sky, and went in with a naked soul.

They walked across it in silence, well apart from each other. When they came out the other side, Mrs. Gustus said, "We must stay for a little while within reach of this. It has something. . ."

Mr. Russell swallowed something that he had thought of saying, and instead drew his Hound's attention to a yellow square of mustard-field which made brilliant the distance.

Kew said nothing, but he felt choked with a lost remembrance of a very old childhood. He seemed to taste the quiet taste of youth here, there was even a feeling of going home through a damp evening to a nursery tea. It was the nursery of all Secret Worlds. Gods had been born there. No surprise could live there now, no wonder, no protest. The years like minutes fled between those trees, dynasties might fall during the singing of a bird. I think the thing that haunted the wood was a thing exactly as old and as romantic as the first child that tracked its Secret Friend across the floor of a forest.

Oh, friend of childlike mind, what is it that these two years have taken from us, what is it that we have lost, oh friend, besides contentment?

All the way home Kew sang very loudly the first tune he ever knew.

When the Family (including Mr. Russell) got back to the inn, the lamb and the gooseberry tart and Cousin Gustus were all waiting for them. But they were delayed in the hall. A stout young woman with a pleasant face of small vocabulary turned from the visitors' book and stopped Mrs. Gustus.

"Are you THE Mrs. Augustus Martin?" she asked.

"I am she," replied Anonyma. Her grammar in moments of emergency always impressed Kew.

I cannot say that Mrs. Gustus seemed surprised. She was the sort of person to hide even from herself the fact that this thing had never happened before. She remained perfectly calm as if repeating a hackneyed experience. Kew was astonished. Mr. Russell shared this feeling. Having a certain personal admiration for Mrs. Gustus, he had tried on more than one occasion to find pleasure in her books, but without success.

The stout young lady said nothing more than "Oh" for the moment, but she breathed it in such a manner that Mrs. Gustus saw at once the duty of asking her to dine with the Family.

When the admirer was introduced to Cousin Gustus, she said, "Oh, so this is your husband. . ." and gazed on that melancholy man with eagerness. When she saw Mr. Russell's Hound she said, "And this is your dog," and was about to crown him with a corresponding halo when Mrs. Gustus disclaimed the connection.

"It is wonderful to meet you, of all people, in this romantic place," said the admirer as she pursued her peas. "Do you know, whenever I finish one of your books, I feel so romantic I want to kiss everybody I meet. Oh, those courtly heroes of yours!"

A heavy silence fell for a moment.

"And your descriptions of nature," continued the admirer. "That sunset seen from the west coast of Ireland that you describe in *The Courtship of Hartley Casey*. You must know Ireland very well."

"I have never been there," said Mrs. Gustus. "I evolve my scenery. After all, Nature lives in the heart of each one of us. I think we all have a sort of Secret World of our own, out of which all that is best in us comes. One does not need to see with one's outward eyes."

"Oh, goodness me, how true that is," said the admirer. "But you must write a book about the downs, won't you? Do you take notes on your travels?"

"My notebook is never out of my hand," answered Mrs. Gustus. "I jot down whatever occurs to me, wherever I may be. I write by moonlight in the night, I have had to pause in the middle of my prayers in Church, I have stood transfixed in the full flow of a London street. I always hope that people will think I am suddenly remembering that I forgot to order tomorrow's dinner."

But really she knew that no one could ever be deceived in the purpose of the notebook.

"Oh, mustn't it be wonderful!" breathed the admirer, and Cousin Gustus, who was always properly impressed by his wife when the example was set by strangers, nodded with a proprietary smile. "And are you writing now?" she continued.

"I am always writing," said Mrs. Gustus, who had seldom enjoyed herself so much, "my pen never rests. A lifetime is too short to allow of rest. But I am not here primarily for inspiration. We are on a quest."

"Oh, how romantic," moaned the admirer.

"It is a quest with a certain amount of romance in it," agreed Anonyma. "We are seeking a House By The Sea. We know very little about it except that it exists. We know that its windows look west, and that the sun sets over the sea. We know that it stands ungardened on the cliff and has a great view. We know that it is seven hundred years old, and full of inspiration. . ."

"We know," continued Kew, "that you can—and often do—drop a fishing-line out of the window into the sea when you are tired of playing the goldfish in the water-butt. We know that the owner of the house is a rotten shot, and that the stone balls from the balustrade are not at this moment where they ought to be. We know that aeroplanes as well as seagulls nest in those cliffs. . ."

"We know—" began Mr. Russell, but this was too much for Mrs. Gustus. After all, the lady was her admirer.

"What's all this?" said Mrs. Gustus. "What do you people know about it?"

"I just thought I would talk a little now," said Kew. "I get quickly tired of hearing other people giving information without help from me."

"At any rate, Russ," continued Mrs. Gustus, "you can't know anything whatever about the matter. You have hardly listened when I read Jay's letters."

"I told you that I remembered," said Mr. Russell. "I don't know how. I remember sitting on a high cliff and seeing three black birds swim in a row, and dive in a row, and in a row come up again after I had counted hundreds."

"Nonsense," said Mrs. Gustus, trying not to appear cross before the visitor, "you're thinking of something else. You can see such a sight as that at the Zoo any day."

"You all seem to know quite a lot about the place," said the admirer, "yet not much of a very practical nature, if I may say so."

"Everything practical is unromantic," said Mrs. Gustus. "There is nothing true or beautiful in the world but poetry. If we seek in real simplicity of mind, we shall find what we seek, for simplicity is poetry, and poetry is truth."

"Also, of course, England has only one west coast," added Kew, "and if we don't find the place we shall have found a good many other things by the time we have finished."

"It may be in Ireland," suggested the admirer.

"No, because she answers our letters so quickly."

"She?"

"My young cousin, the object of our search."

"Did she run away?" asked the admirer, in a voice strangled with excitement.

To admit that a young relation of Anonyma's should run away from her would be undignified.

"You mustn't take us too seriously," said Mrs. Gustus lightly. "It isn't a case of an elopement, or anything like that. Just an excuse for a tour, and a rest from wearisome war work. A wild-goose chase, nothing but fun in it."

"Wild goose is a good description of Jay," said Cousin Gustus. It was rather.

Next morning the admirer, twittering with excitement, came in upon the Family while it was having its breakfast.

"Oh, I had such an idea in the night," she said. "I couldn't sleep, of course, after such an exciting day. I believe I have been fated to help you in your quest. I know of a house near here, and the more I think of it the more sure I feel that it is the place you want."

"Who lives there?"

"A young man with his mother. I forget the name."

"Place we want's west," objected Mr. Russell.

"You never can tell," said Anonyma. "This place may stand on a salient, facing west. Our search must be thorough."

"It's such a lovely walk," said the admirer. "I should be so much honoured if you would let me show you the way. Oh, I say, do you think me very presumptuous?"

Her self-consciousness took the form of a constant repentance. In the night she would go over her day and probe it for tender points. "Oh, that was a dreadful thing to say," was a refrain that would keep her awake for hours, wriggling and giggling in her bed over the dreadfulness of it. She had too little egoism. The lack gave her face a look of littleness. A lack of altruism has the same outward effect. A complete face should be full of something, of gentleness, of vigour, of humour, of wickedness. The admirer's face was only half full of anything. All the same there was charm about her, the fact that she was an admirer was charming. Mrs. Gustus reassured her.

"We shall be most grateful for a guide."

"We should be even more grateful for an excuse to call on this inoffensive young man and his mother at eleven o'clock in the morning," objected Kew.

"He ought to be at the Front," was the excuse provided by Cousin Gustus.

"So ought I," sighed Kew.

"Oh, but you're a wounded, aren't you?" asked the admirer. There were signs of a possible transfer of admiration, and Mrs. Gustus interposed with presence of mind.

"We'll start," she said. "Don't let's be hampered in the beginning of our quest by social littleness."

She was conscious that she looked handsome enough for any breach of convention. She wore an unusual shaped dress the colour of vanilla ice. Instead of doing her hair as usual in one severe penny bun at the back, she had constructed a halfpenny bun, so to speak, over each ear. This is a very literary way of doing the hair, and the remembrance of the admirer, haunting Anonyma's waking thoughts, had inspired the change.

Their way lay through the beechwood that embroiders the hem of the down's cloak. There are only two colours in a beechwood after rain, lilac and green. A bank of violets is not more pure in colour than a beech trunk shining in the sun. The two colours answered one another, fainter and fainter, away and away, to the end of one's sight, and there were two cuckoos, hidden in the dream, mocking each other in velvet voices. The view between the trees was made up of horizons that tilted one's chin. The bracken, very young, on an opposite slope, was like a cloud of green wings alighting. But the look of their destination disappointed them.

"This house faces south," said Kew.

"I feel sure—" began Mr. Russell, but Mrs. Gustus said:

"As we are here, we might ask. To be sure, the cliff is rather tame."

"But there is an aeroplane," persisted the admirer.

"Now pause, Anonyma," Kew warned her. "Pause and consider what you are going to say."

"Consideration only unearths difficulties," laughed Anonyma. "Best go forward in faith and fearlessness."

She was under the impression that she constantly laughed in a nicely naughty way at Kew's excessive conventionality.

As they drew nearer to the cliff, it grew tamer and tamer. The house, too, became dangerously like a villa; a super-villa, to be sure, and not in its first offensive youth, but still closely connected with the villa tribe. Its complexion was a bilious yellow, and it had red-rimmed windows. It was close to the sea, however, and its windows, with their blinds drawn down against the sun, looked like eyes downcast towards the beach.

There was no lodge, and the Family walked in silence through the gate. Mr. Russell's Hound went first with a defiant expression about his tail. That expression cost him dear. Inside the gate there stood a large vulgar dog, without a tail to speak of. Its parting was crooked, its hair was in its eyes. All these personal disadvantages the Family had time to note, while the dog gazed incredulously at Mr. Russell's Hound.

A Pekinese dog never wears country clothes. It always looks as if it had its silk hat and spats on. If I were a country dog, who had never even smelt a Piccadilly smell, I should certainly bite all dogs of the type of Mr. Russell's Hound.

I could hardly describe what followed as a fight. Although I have always loved stories of giant-killers, from David downwards, and should much like to write one, I cannot in this case pretend that Mr. Russell's Hound did anything but call for help. Anonyma's umbrella, Kew's cane, and Mr. Russell's stick did all they could towards making peace, but the big dog seemed to have set itself the unkind task of mopping up a puddle with Mr. Russell's Hound. The process took a considerable time. And it was never finished, for the mistress of the house interrupted it.

She was rather a fat person, apparently possessing the gift of authority, for the sound of her call reached her dog through the noise of battle. He saw that his aim was not one to achieve in the presence of an audience. He disengaged his teeth from the mane of Mr. Russell's Hound.

"Is your dog much hurt?" asked the mistress of the house, and handed Anonyma a slate.

Anonyma scanned this unexpected gift nervously. She was much more used to taking other people aback than to being taken aback herself. But Kew was more ready. He dived for the pencil and wrote, "Only a bit punctured," on the slate.

"You'd better bring it in and bathe it," suggested the lady, when she had studied this.

They followed her in silent single file. Anonyma noticed that her hair was apparently done in imitation of a pigeon's nest, also that many hooks at the back of her dress had lost their grip of the situation.

The bathroom, whither Mr. Russell's Hound was carried, was suggestive of another presence in the house. A boat, called *Golden Mary*, was navigating the bath. There were some prostrate soldiers and chessmen in a little heap on the ledge, apparently waiting for a passage.

"I'm getting out my son's things because he is coming home," said the lady.

Mr. Russell was bathing his bleeding Hound in the basin, and Anonyma was at the window, ostentatiously drinking in the view. Kew took the slate and wrote politely on it: "From school?"

"From the War," said the lady.

Kew donned a pleased and interested expression. It seemed to him better to do this than to write, "Really!" on the slate.

"He wrote about a fortnight ago," the lady's harsh voice continued, "to say he would come today. He said he was sick of being grown-up, he told me to get out the soldiers and the *Golden Mary*. He wants to launch them on the pond again."

Kew nodded. "I have felt like that," he murmured, and the lady seemed to see the sense of his words.

"I should think you are six years older than Murray," she said, "and very different. Come out into the garden, and I'll show you."

Kew followed her, and Anonyma, after a moment's hesitation, went too. But Mr. Russell, who had finished his work of mercy, seemed to think it better to linger in the bathroom, explaining to his Hound the subject of a Biblical picture which hung over the bath.

"You might think I was rather too old to play things well," the mother said to Kew. "But you should see me with Murray. Even my deafness never hindered me with him, I could always see what he said. Look, we made this road for the soldiers coming down to the wharf. Do you see the way we helped nature, by tampering with the roots of the beech. It is a perfect wharf, this little flat bit, it is just level with the deck of the boat at high tide. The lower wharf is for low tide, but of course we have to pretend the tides. That round place is the bandstand, and there the pipers play when there is a troop-ship starting. Sometimes only the Favourite Piper plays, striding up and down the little bowling-green at the top here, but not often, because the work of keeping him going interferes with the disembarkation. We never let the Highlanders go abroad, because Murray loves them so. He is afraid lest something should happen to them. Were the Highlanders your favourites?"

Kew wrote on the slate: "No, the Egyptian Camel Corps."

The lady nodded. "We loved them too, but of course they lived on the other side of the pond, and sometimes they and the Sepoys and the Soudanese had to insurrect. Somebody had to, you know, but we regretted the Egyptian Camel Corps awfully. I hope you don't think us silly. . . Murray was always a childish person. I hope I am too. The bowling-green gave us a lot of trouble to make; it is nice and flat, isn't it? We trim it with nail-scissors."

It was a good bowling-green, about twelve inches by six. There were some marbles on it.

"It has historical associations," said the mother of Murray. "It was here that Drake played when the Armada was sighted. Of course that was before our time, but sometimes, on a moonlit summer night, we used to lie down on our fronts and see his little ghost haunting the green. We used to bring our young sailors here, and inspire them with stories about Drake. The sailors used to stand on the green, and we put up railings made of matches all round, and civilians used to stand in great breathless crowds outside the railings watching. Chessmen, of course. Murray used to make the civilians arrive in motors, so as to make ruts in the road. Somehow it was always rather splendid and real to have ruts in the road."

There was a long pause.

"Later on, of course, things got more grown-up. The last time we played before the War—when War was already in sight—we shipped an unprecedented mass of troops to that peninsula, and had a wonderful battle. You can still see the trenches and gun emplacements; I cleared them out yesterday. Murray joined the Army in that first August, and whenever he came home after that he was somehow ashamed of these things. I quite understood that. When I am having tea with the Vicar's wife, or cutting out shirts for the soldiers, I sometimes blush a little to think how old I am, and to think of the things I do at home with Murray. I am sure he felt just the same when he was with other men. But his last letter was young again. He wrote that the War should cease the moment he set foot inside this gate, and we would have a civilian game, an alpine expedition up the mountains. You see the beech-root mountains. There is the cave where we put up for the night. There is a wonderful view from Bumpy Peak, over the sea, and right away to far-off lands. Murray thought that when the expedition had caught a chamois it might turn into engineers prospecting for the building of a road up to Bumpy Peak, so that the soldiers might march up, and look out over the sea, and see—very far off—the fringes of the East that they had conquered, when they were young and not tired of War. . ."

She broke off and looked at Kew.

Anonyma stood a few paces away, gazing at her vanilla-ice reflection in the pond.

"I dare say you think us silly," said the lady. "I dare say you would think Murray a rotter if you met him. It doesn't matter much. It doesn't matter at all. Nothing matters, because he will come home tonight."

Kew fidgeted a moment, and then took the slate and wrote: "I am very much afraid that all leave from abroad has been stopped this week."

"Yes, I know," said the mother, "I have been unhappy about that for some days. But it doesn't make any difference to Murray now. You see,

I heard last night that he was killed on Tuesday. That's why I know he will come, and I shall be waiting here. Can't you imagine them shouting as they get through, as they get through with being grown-up, shouting to each other as they run back to their childhood and their old pretences. . ."

After a moment she added, "That is the only sound that I shall ever hear now,—the shouting of Murray to me as he runs home."

It was in a sort of dream that Kew watched Anonyma go forward and take both the hands of the mother. I suppose he knew that all that was superfluous, and that Murray would come home.

Anonyma said, "I am so sorry. I am so sorry that we intruded. You must forgive us."

The mother of Murray did not hear, but she saw that sympathy was intended, and she nodded awkwardly, and a little severely. I don't think she had known that Anonyma was there.

Kew was not sorry that he had intruded.

At sunset, when the high sea span
About the rocks a web of foam,
I saw the ghost of a Cornishman
Come home.
I saw the ghost of a Cornishman
Run from the weariness of War,
I heard him laughing as he ran
Across his unforgotten shore.
The great cliff, gilded by the west,
Received him as an honoured guest.
The green sea, shining in the bay,
Did drown his dreadful yesterday.

Come home, come home, you million ghosts,
The honest years shall make amends,
The sun and moon shall be your hosts,
The everlasting hills your friends.
And some shall seek their mothers' faces,
And some shall run to trysting-places,
And some to towns, and others yet
Shall find great forests in their debt.
    Oh, I would siege the golden coasts
    Of space, and climb high heaven's dome,
    So I might see those million ghosts
    Come home.

Next day all the Family, including Mr. Russell and excepting Cousin Gustus, came to breakfast with the intention of announcing that he or she must go up to London by the next train. Mrs. Gustus, as ever, spoke first.

"My conscience is pricking me. My work is calling me. I must go up and see my old darlings in the Brown Borough. There is, I see, a train at ten."

"I was just going to say something quite different to the same effect," said Kew. "I want to go up and whisper some secrets into the ear of Cox. I want to have my hair cut. I want to buy this week's *Punch*. I want some brown bootlaces. Life is empty for me unless I go up to town this morning."

Mr. Russell, although he had tried the effect of all his excuses on his Hound while dressing, was silent.

Mrs. Gustus was never less than half an hour too early for trains. This might account for the excellence of her general information. She had spent a large portion of her life at railway stations, which are, I think, the centre of much wisdom. She and Kew started for the station with mouths burnt by hurried coffee and toast-crumbs still unbrushed on their waistcoats, forty minutes before the train was due. The protests of Kew could be heard almost as far as the station, which was reached by a walk of five minutes.

Cousin Gustus, Mr. Russell, and the convalescent Hound went to lie upon the downs which climbed up straight from the back doorstep of the inn. They were accompanied by a rug, a scarf, a sunshade, an overcoat, the blessings of the landlady, and Cousin Gustus's diary. Nobody ever knew what sort of matter filled Cousin Gustus's diary, nobody ever wanted to know. It gave him grounds for claiming literary tastes, and his literary tastes presumably made him marry a literary wife. So the diary had a certain importance.

They spread out the rug in a little hollow, like a giant's footprint in the downs, and sheep and various small flowers looked over their shoulders.

For the first ten minutes Mr. Russell lay on his back listening to the busy sound of the bees filling their honeybags, and the sheep filling themselves, and Cousin Gustus filling his diary. He watched the rooks travel across the varied country of the sky. He watched a little black and white bird that danced in the air to the tune of its own very high and flippant song. He watched the sun ford a deep and foaming cloud. And all the time he remembered many reasons why it would have been nice to go up to London. Oddly enough, a 'bus-conductor seemed to stand quite apart from these reasons in the back of his mind for several minutes. One would hardly have believed that a bus-conductor could have held her own so long in the mind of a person like Mr. Russell.

And Providence finally ordained that he should feel in his cigarette case and find it empty.

"No cigarettes," said Mr. Russell, after pondering for a moment on this disappointment.

"You smoke too much," said Cousin Gustus. "I once knew a man who over-smoked all his life, and when he got a bullet in his lung in the Zulu War he died, simply as the result of his foolishness. No recuperative power. They said his lungs were simply leather."

"Should have thought that would've been a protection," said Mr. Russell.

"The train is not even signalled yet," said Cousin Gustus. "You would have time to go to the station and tell Kew to get you some cigarettes."

But this was not Providence's intention, as interpreted by Mr. Russell. "D'you know, I half believe I'll go up too," he said. "Would you be lonely?"

"Not in the least," said Cousin Gustus pathetically; "I'm used to being left alone."

As the signals dropped Mr. Russell sprang to his feet and ran down the slope. He had country clothes on, and some thistledown and a sprig or two of clover were sticking to them. He reached the station in time, and fell over a crate of hens. The hens were furious about it, and said so. Mr. Russell said nothing, but he felt hurt when the porter who opened the door for him asked if the hens were his. After the train had started he wished he had had time to tell the porter how impossible it was that a man who owned a crate full of hens should fall over it. And then he thought that would have been neither witty nor convincing. He was one of those lucky people who say so little that they rarely have need to regret what they have said.

The business that dragged him so precipitately from the country must, I suppose, have been very urgent. It chanced that it lay at Ludgate Circus, and it also chanced—not in the least unnaturally—that at half-past eleven he was standing at Kensington Church waiting to be beckoned to once more by a 'bus-conductor. The only unnatural thing was that several 'buses bound for Ludgate Circus passed without winning the patronage of Mr. Russell.

The conductor came. Mr. Russell saw her round face and squared hair appear out of the confusion of the street. He noticed with surprise that he had not borne in mind the pleasing way in which the strap of her hat tilted her already tilted chin.

Jay had been thinking a little about Mr. Russell, not much. She had been wondering who he was. The Family's friends and relations were always much talked of in the Family, and much invited, and much met. Mr. Russell had not been among them when Jay had last known the Family. An idea was in her mind that he might be a private detective, engaged by the Family to seek out their fugitive young relation. Mr. Russell had plainly alluded to a search. Jay had no experience of private detectives, but she thought it quite possible that they might disguise themselves with rather low foreheads, and rather frowning eyes, and shut thin mouths, and shut thin expressions. She hoped that she would see him today. An hour ago a young man with a spotty complexion and bulging eyes like a rabbit's had handed her a note with his threepence, asking for a "two-and-a-half" in a lovelorn voice. She handed him back his halfpenny and his unopened note at once, saying, "Your change, sir," in a kind, absent-minded voice. I am afraid an incident like this is always a little exciting, though I admit it ought to be insulting. That suggestive fare made Jay hope more and more that she would meet Mr. Russell today. I don't exactly know why, except that sentimentality is an infectious complaint.

Mr. Russell got happily into the 'bus. He made the worst entrance possible. His hat slipped crooked, he left one leg behind on the road, and only retrieved it with the help of the conductor. Jay welcomed him with a nod that was almost a bow, a remnant of her unprofessional past.

"Told you I'd come in this 'bus again," said Mr. Russell, sitting down in the left-hand seat next to the door. I really don't know what would have happened if that seat had been occupied. I suppose Mr. Russell would have sat upon the occupier.

"A good many people like this service," said Jay; "it is considered very convenient. How is your search going?"

"It hasn't begun yet," said Mr. Russell. "We haven't got within three hundred miles of the House we're looking for."

"You know more or less where it is, then?" asked Jay, who sometimes wanted to know this herself.

"I do know, but I don't know how I know, nor what I know."

"How funny that you—an Older and Wiser Man—should feel that sort of knowledge," said Jay. As an afterthought she called him Sir.

The 'bus grew fuller, and only Jay's bell punctured the silence that followed. A lady asked Jay to "set her down at Charing Cross Post Office." "The 'bus stops there automatically, Madam," said Jay, and the lady told her not to be impertinent.

Jay seemed a little subdued after this, and it was only after she had stood for a minute or two on her platform in silence that she said to Mr. Russell, "London seems dead today, doesn't it? Not even fog, only a lifeless light. What's the use of daylight in London today? You know, I don't live in London."

"No," said Mr. Russell, "where do you live?"

"London," replied Jay. "I mean my heart doesn't live in London mostly. I think it lives very far away in the same sort of place as the place you know without knowing how you know it. The happy shore of God Knows Where must have a great population of hearts. Today I hate London so that I could tear it into pieces like a rag."

"You ought to start your 'bus on the search for the happy shore," said Mr. Russell. "You'd find the track of my tyres before you. I b'lieve you'd find the place."

"Well, that would be the only perfect Service," said Jay. "But I don't believe the public would use the route much. I would go on and on, and leave all old ruts behind. I would stop for no fares, even the sea should not stop me. I would go on to the horizon to see if that secret look just after sunset really means that the stars are just over the brink. Why do people end themselves on a note of despair? I would choose that way of perpetuating my Perfect Day. The police would see the top seats of the 'bus sticking out at low tide, and the verdict would be, 'Suicide while of even more than usually unsound mind.'"

A 'bus has an unromantic voice. The bass is a snarl, and the treble is made up of a shrill rattle. It was curious how this 'bus managed to retain withal its fantastic atmosphere.

Mr. Russell asked presently, "Why are you a 'bus-conductor?"

"To get some money," replied the conductor baldly. "I want to find out what is the attraction of money. Besides, if one talks such a lot as I do, to do anything—however small—saves one from being utterly futile.

When I get to Heaven, the angels won't be able to say, 'Tush tush, you lived on the charity of God.' That's what unearned money is, isn't it? And what's the use of charity?"

"Do you ever get a day off?" asked Mr. Russell.

"Occasionally."

"Will you meet me on the steps of St. Paul's next Sunday at ten?"

"No, because I shall be at work next Sunday."

"Will you meet me the Sunday after that?"

"Yes," said Jay. The Family's theories on the bringing up of girls had evidently been wasted on her.

"What's the use of looking for this girl?" she asked, after a round of duty. "Why not leave her on her happy shore? Do you know, sir, I sympathise enormously with that girl."

"I don't expect you would if you knew her," said Mr. Russell. "She must be quite different from you, by what I hear from her relations. I think she must be an aggressive, suffragetty sort of girl. Girls nowadays seem to find running away from home a sufficient profession."

"You say that because you are so dreadfully much Older and Wiser," said Jay. "Why are you looking for her, then?"

"I'm not," said Mr. Russell. "She is just a trespasser. I'm looking for the place because I know I know it."

"I hope you'll never find it," said Jay crossly. She announced Ludgate Circus in a startling voice, and ended the conversation.

She was tired because she had been up all night among distressed friends in the Brown Borough. There had been a fight in Tann Street. Mrs. O'Rourke had broken the face of little Mrs. Love. Mrs. Love had never fought before; her fists were like lamb cutlets, and she had had a good mother with non-combatant principles. All these things are drawbacks in a Brown Borough argument. But Mrs. Love was a friend of Jay's, and I don't think she had found that a drawback. Feverish discussions with dreadfully impartial policemen, feverish drying of feverish tears, feverish extracting of medicaments from closed chemists, and finally a feverish triumph of words with which Jay capped Mrs. O'Rourke's triumph of fists were the items in the sum of a feverish night. So Jay was tired.

Mr. Russell was too early for his business, and he went into St. Paul's and sat on a seat far back.

St. Paul was an anti-saint, I think, who very badly needed to get married and be answered back now and then. I believe it is possible that he was unworthy of that great house called by his name. The gospel of a very splendid detachment speaks within its walls, its windows turn inward, its music sings to itself. Tossed City sinners go in and out, and pass, and penetrate, but still the music dreams, and still the dim gold blinks above their heads. A muffled God walks the aisles, and you, in the bristling wilderness of chairs, can clutch at His skirts and never see His eyes. Nothing comes forward from that altar to meet you. It is as if He walked talking to Himself, and as if even His speech were lost in those devouring spaces.

Mr. Russell sat near the door, and found only his thoughts and the shuffle of seeking feet to keep him company.

"An Older and Wiser Man. . ." he thought. "God forgive me for letting it pass."

If he had thought it worth while to profess an "ism" at all, he would have been a fatalist. He was the victim of an unwitty cynicism, and of a heavy irresponsibility. He applied either "It isn't worth while" or "It doesn't matter" to everything. He never expressed his thoughts to himself—it was not worth while,—but I think he knew within himself that life was made of paper, and thrown together in a crackling chaos. There was no depth in anything, and a mere thought could slay the highest thing in the world. The only thing that ever made his heart laugh was the idea of fineness finding place in himself. A dream of himself in a heroic light sometimes made him poke himself in the ribs, and mock the farce of human vanity. He was like a man in a world that lacked mirrors, a man who sees his dark deformed shadow on the sands, and thinks it represents him fairly.

He was without self-consciousness, knowing that he was not worth his own recognition. At home he often recited little confused poems of his own composition to his Hound, and never noticed the surprise of the servants. He never knew that in the company of Mr. and Mrs. Gustus and Kew he was hardly allowed to utter three consecutive words, although, when he was away from them, and especially when he was with the 'bus-conductor, he felt a delightful lack of restraint.

As he sat down and looked at the far unanswering altar, he had two dim thoughts. One was that a man might get Older and Wiser, without getting old enough or wise enough to choose his road. The other was a question as to whether it is ever really worth while to read what the signpost says.

From the moment when Mr. Russell left her 'bus, Jay became stupefied by an invasion of the Secret World.

She gave the tickets and change with accuracy, she kept count of the stream of climbers on to the top of the 'bus, she stilled the angry whirlpool of people on the pavement for whom there was no room, she dislodged passengers at the corners of their own streets—even that gentleman (almost always to be found in an obscure corner of an east-going 'bus) who had sunk into a sudden and pathetic sleep just when his pennyworth of ride was coming to an end,—she received an unexpected inspector with the smile that comes of knowing every passenger to be properly ticketed; she even laughed at his joke. She weeded out the Whitechapel Jewesses at the Bank, and introduced them to the Mile End 'buses. She handed out to them their sombre and insolent-looking babies, and when one mother thanked her profusely in Yiddish, she replied, "Bitte, bitte. . ." Yet all the while the wind blew to her old remembrances of the low chimneys and the bending roofs of the House by the Sea, and the smell of the high curving fields, and the shouting of the sea. And all the while her hands must grope for the handle of the heavy door, and her eyes must fill with blindness because of the wonderful promise of distant cliffs with the sun on them, and because the sea was so shining. And all the while her ears must strain to hear a voice within the house. . .

It is a very great honour to be given two lives to live.

The monotonous journeys trod on each other's heels. Slowly the day consumed itself. It grew dimmer and dimmer for Jay, though I have no doubt that habit protected her, and that she behaved herself throughout with commonplace correctness.

She found presently that the great weight of copper money was gone from her shoulder, and that it was evening, and that Chloris was coming down Mabel Place to meet her. Chloris was wagging her whole person from the shoulder-blades backwards; she never found adequate the tail that had originally been provided for that purpose. Jay stumbled up the step of Eighteen Mabel Place, and found at last the path she wanted.

The path was one that had never been touched by a professional pathmaker. Feet, not hands, had made it. The rocks impatiently thrust it aside every little way, and here and there were steps up and down for no reason except that the rock would have it so. The path chose its way so that you might see the sea from every inch of it. The thundering headlands sprang from Jay's left hand, and she could see the cliffs written over with strange lines, and the shadow that they cast upon deep water. It was the colour of a great passion, and against that colour pink foxgloves bowed dramatically upon the fringe of space. The white gulls were in the valleys of the sea. I wish colour could be built by words. I wish I could speak colour to myself in the dark. I can never fill my eyes full enough of the colour of the sea, nor my ears of the crying of the seagulls. I am most greedy of these things, and take no thought for the morrow, so that if my morrow dawns darkly I have nothing stored away to comfort me.

The path joins the more civilised road almost at the door of the House by the Sea. You tumble over a great round rock that still bears the marks of the sea's fingers, and you are at the door.

The house was full of sunlight. Great panels of sunlight lay across the air. The fingers of the honeysuckle in the rough painted bowl by the window caught and held sunlight. In every room of the house you can always hear the eternal march of the sea up and down the shore. Nothing ever drowns that measured confusion. Sometimes the voices of friends thread in and out of it, sometimes the dogs bark, or a coming meal clinks in the stone passage, or you can catch the squealing of the children in their baths, sometimes your heart stops beating to listen to the speech of the ghosts that haunt the house, but no sound ever usurps the throne of the sea.

They were all on the stairs, the Secret Friend and the children. They all wore untidy clothes, and hard-boiled eggs bulged from their pockets. The Secret Friend has red hair, you might call its colour vulgar. But Jay likes it very much. He hardly ever sits still, you can never see him think, he has a way of answering you almost before you have finished speaking. His mind always seems to be exploring among words, and sometimes you can hear him telling himself splendid sentences without meaning. For this reason everything connected with him has a name, from his dog, which is called Trelawney, to the last cigarette he smokes at night, which is called Isobel. This trick Jay has imported into her own establishment: she has an umbrella called Macdonald, and a little occasional pleurisy pain under one rib, which she introduces to the Family as Julia.

The children in the house were just those very children that every woman hopes, or has hoped, to have for her own.

They were just starting for a walk, and the Secret Friend was finishing a story.

"How can you remember things that happened—I suppose—squillions of years ago," said the eldest child. "You tell them as if they happened yesterday. Doesn't it seem as if all the happiest things happened yesterday?"

"To me it seems that they will happen tomorrow," said the Secret Friend. "But then there is so little difference between yesterday and tomorrow. How can you tell which is which? Only clocks and calendars are silly enough to tread on the tail of a little space between sunrise and sunset and call it today. How do you know which way up time is happening?"

"Because yesterday the sun set, and we went to bed," said the youngest child.

"I think tomorrow is a little person in dark clothes watching and listening," said the eldest child. "And today is Cinderella, all shiny and beautiful until twelve o'clock strikes."

"All yesterdays and all tomorrows are in this house listening," said the Secret Friend. "This is the place where time is without a name. Here the beginning comes after the end. Tomorrow we shall be born. Yesterday we died. Today was just a little passage built of twenty-four odd hours. And now we will sing the Loud Song."

They were on the rocky path now, and they sang the Loud Song. Both that path and that song go on for ever, and the words of the song are like this:

> *There is no house like our house*
> *Even in Heaven.*
> *There is no family like our family*
> *Even in Heaven.*
> *There is no Country like our Country*
> *Even in Heaven.*
> *There is no sea like our sea*
> *Even in Heaven.*

Most families sing this song, more or less, but few could sing it so loudly as this family did.

The dog Trelawney ran after the shadows of the seagulls.

There is the track my feet have worn
By which my fate may find me:
From that dim place where I was born
Those footprints run behind me.
Uncertain was the trail I left,
For—oh, the way was stormy;
But now this splendid sea has cleft
My journey from before me.

Three things the sea shall never end,
Three things shall mock its power:
My singing soul, my Secret Friend,
And this my perfect hour.

And you shall seek me till you reach
The tangled tide advancing,
And you shall find upon the beach
The traces of my dancing,
And in the air the happy speech
Of Secret Friends romancing.

For some minutes some one had been knocking on the door. The sound was like an intruder in the Secret World, beckoning insistently to Jay. But she took no notice of it until a loud voice said: "You need not think you are paddling in golden seas and inaccessible to your relations, because you are here, and I can see you through the window."

After a moment's confusion, Jay found that this was so, and she got up and let Kew in.

"I will just ask you how you are," he said hurriedly. "And how things are going in the Other World, and all that. But you needn't answer, because I haven't much time, and I want very badly to talk about myself. I never get a chance when Anonyma is there, and when I return to France (which is likely to happen soon), I shan't find much chance to talk there. I am so glad I am going back, I am so sick of hearing other people talk about things that are not worth mentioning. Poor dear Anonyma, she meant all this recent gaiety as a reward to me for war work dutifully done. But if this be jam, give me my next pill unadorned. A motor tour combined with Anonyma is tiring. If I were alone with Russ I might enjoy it."

"Who is Russ?"

"The owner of Christina, and Christina is the vehicle which contains us during the search for you."

He became aware of the velvet face of Chloris, gazing at him from between his knees.

"What does Chloris do while you are week-ending in Heaven. Do you take her with you?"

"There is already a dog there, called Trelawney."

"By Jove, that would make a nice little clue for Anonyma. There can be only one dog on the sea-coast called Trelawney. We could stop and ask every dog we met what its name was. Besides, the name suggests Cornwall. What breed is the dog? Look here, will you write the Family a letter giving it a few neat clues for Anonyma? After all, we ought to give her all the pleasure we can, I sometimes think we are a disappointing family for her to have married. We lie to her, she lies to us, her enthusiasms make us smile behind our hands, ours make her yawn behind her notebook. Send us a good encouraging letter, addressed to the house in Kensington. We always wire our address there as we move. Give us details about Trelawney, and, if possible, the name of the nearest post town. If we must lie, let us give all the pleasure we can by doing so. Poor old Anonyma.

"It's getting dark, I must go back to the Family. I am as a babe in the hands of Anonyma, and like a babe I promised her I would be back before dark. Do you remember how we used to long to be lost after nightfall, just for the dramatic effect? Yet we were awfully frightened of the dark. Do you remember how we used to dare each other to get out of bed and run three times round the night nursery? I have never felt so brave since, as I used to feel as I jumped into bed conscious of an ordeal creditably over. Why is bed such a safe place? I am not half so brave as I used to be. I remember at the age of ten doing a thing that I have never dared to do since. I sat in the bath with my back to the taps. Do you suppose the innocent designer of baths meant everybody to sit like that, with a tap looking over each shoulder? Taps are known to be savage brutes, and it is everybody's instinct to sit the other way round, and keep an eye on the danger. If I were as brave now as I was at ten, I could probably win the War. Oh, Jay, I can't stop talking, I am so pleased to be nearly out of the clutches of my relations."

"Are you sure you won't be killed?" asked Jay suddenly.

"I can't be," said Kew. "How could I be? I'm me. I'm not brave, and I don't go to France with one eye on duty and the other on the possibility of never coming back. I go because the crowd goes, and the crowd—a rather shrunken crowd—will come back safe. I'm too average a man to get killed."

"Don't you think all those million ghosts are thinking, 'What business had Death to choose me?'" suggested Jay.

"No," said Kew. "I'm sure they know."

After a few seconds' pause he said, "By Jove, are you in fancy dress?"

"No. Why?"

"Why indeed. Why a kilt and yards of gaiters? Why a hat like a Colonial horse marine?"

"Oh, this is the uniform of a bus-conductor," replied Jay.

Kew scanned it with distaste. Presently he said, "Don't you think you'd better give it up? Buy a new hat with a day's earnings, and get the sack."

"I can't quarrel with my bread and butter," said Jay.

"Surely this is only jam," said Kew. "You've got plenty of money of your own for bread and butter."

"I haven't now," answered Jay. "I gave up having money when the War started. Perhaps I chucked it into the Serpentine. Perhaps not. I forget."

STELLA BENSON

Kew got up slowly. "Well," he said, "sure you're all right? I must be going. I don't know when the last train goes."

In London it is impossible to ignore the fact that you are late. The self-righteous hands of clocks point out your guilt whichever way you look. Your eye and your ear are accused on every side. You long for the courteous clocklessness of the country; there, mercifully, the sun neither ticks nor strikes, nor cavils at the minutes.

There was a crowd of home-goers at Brown Borough Church, and each 'bus as it arrived was like the angel troubling the waters of Bethesda. There was no hope for the old or timid. Kew was an expert in the small sciences of London. He knew not only how to mount a 'bus, while others of his like were trying four abreast to do the same, but also how to stand on a space exactly half the size of his boot soles, without holding on. (This is done, as you probably know too, by not looking out of the window.)

Kew had given up taxis and cigars in war-time. It was his pretence never to do anything on principle, so he would have blushed if anybody had commented on this ingenuous economy. The fact that he had joined the Army the first day of the War was also, I think, a tender spot in the conscience of Kew. A Victoria Cross would have been practically unbearable, and even to be mentioned in despatches would have been a most upsetting contradiction of that commonplace and unprincipled past of which he boasted. He thought he was such a simple soul that he had no motives or principles in anything that he did, but really he was simpler than that. He was so simple that he did his best without thinking about it. It certainly sounds rather a curious way to live in the twentieth century.

"'Ere, you're seven standin' inside," said the gentleman 'bus—conductor, when, after long sojourn in upper regions, he came down to his basement floor. "Five standin' is all I'm supposed to 'ave, an' five standin' is all I'll allow. Why should I get myself into trouble for 'avin' more'n five standin', if five standin' is all I'm allowed to 'ave?"

In spite of a chorus of nervous assent from all his flock, and the blushing disappearance of the two superfluous standers, the 'bus-conductor continued his lament in this strain. To the man with a small but loud grievance, sympathy is a fatal offering.

The 'bus-conductor had a round red nose, and very defective teeth. Kew studied him in a new light, for this was Jay's fellow-worker. Somehow it seemed very regrettable.

"I wish I hadn't promised not to tell the Family," he thought.

He and Jay never broke their promises to each other, and there was a tacit agreement that when they found it necessary to lie to each other, they always gave each other warning. Where the rest of the world was concerned, I am afraid they used their discretion in this matter.

"It ought to be stopped. The tactful foot of Family authority ought to step on it."

He presented his penny angrily to the 'bus-conductor.

"I expect this sort of man asks Jay to walk out with him," he thought, and with a cold glance took the ticket offered to him.

"Lucky I'm so utterly selfish," he thought, "or I should be devilish worried."

His train was one which boasted a restaurant car, and Kew patronised this institution. But when he was in the middle of cold meat, he thought: "She is probably trying to live on twopence-halfpenny a week. Continual tripe and onions."

So he refused pudding. The pudding, persistent as only a railway pudding can be, came back incredulously three times. But Kew pushed it away.

"If I could get anybody outside the Family to use their influence, I should be within the letter of the law. But I mostly know subalterns, and nobody below a Brigadier would be likely to have much influence with Jay. She'd probably talk down even a sergeant-major."

It seems curious that he should deplore the fact that Jay had turned into a bus-conductor more deeply than he had deplored her experiments in sweated employment. I think that a uniformed sister or wife is almost unbearable to most men, except, perhaps, one in the nurse's uniform, of which even St. Paul might have approved. The gaiters of the 'bus-conductor had shaken Kew to his foundations. The thought of the skirt still brought his heart into his mouth. He was so lacking in the modern mind that he still considered himself a gentleman. No Socialist, speaking between clenched teeth in a strangled voice of largely groundless protest, had ever gained the ear of Kew. He had never joined a society of any sort. He had never attended a public meeting since he gave up being a Salvationist at the age of ten.

"It must be stopped," he said, as he got out of the train. "I'll think of a way in my bath tomorrow." This was always the moment he looked forward to for inspirations.

Anonyma was observable as he walked from the station to the inn, craning extravagantly from the sitting-room window. She came downstairs, and met him at the door.

"Such a disaster," she said, and handed him a telegram.

Kew stood aghast, as she meant him to. No disaster is ever so great as it is before you know what it is. But Kew ought to have known Anonyma's disasters by experience.

"Russ's wife has appeared."

"Why should she be introduced as a disaster?" asked Kew, with a sigh of relief. "Is she a maniac, or a suffragette, or a Mormon, or just some one who has never read any of your books?"

He opened the telegram. It called upon him to rejoin his battalion next day at noon.

"Russ went to his house to fetch something this morning and found his wife there. He looks quite ill. She insisted on coming here with him, and now she wishes to go on the tour with us. As I hear the car is hers, we can hardly refuse."

"I don't pretend to understand the subtleties of this disaster," said Kew. "But as you evidently don't intend me to, I will not try. Notice, however, that I am keeping my head. I have always wondered how I should behave in a disaster."

"Wait till you meet her," said Anonyma.

Kew heard Mrs. Russell's melodramatic laughter as he approached the sitting-room door, and he trembled. She laughed "Ha-ha-ha" in a concise way, and the sound was constant.

"That is her ready sense of fun that you can hear," said Anonyma bitterly. "She is teaching Gustus to see the humorous side."

They entered to find poor Cousin Gustus bending like a reed before a perfect gale of "Ha-ha-ha's." Mrs. Russell was so much interested in what she was saying that she left Kew on her leeward side for the moment, hardly looking at him as she shook hands.

"It's enough to make the gods laugh on Olympus," she said, but it did not make Cousin Gustus laugh. Noticing this, Mrs. Russell turned to Kew.

"I was telling your cousin about my pacificist efforts in the States," she said. "Yes, I can see your eye twinkling; I know a pacifist is a funny thing to be. But I'm not one of the—what I call dumpy-toad-in-the-hole ones. I do it all joyously. I was telling your cousin how very small was the chance that robbed us of success in Ohio."

"What sort of success?" asked Kew.

"Peace," said Mrs. Russell.

"But is Ohio at war?"

Mrs. Russell laughed heartily. Her unnecessarily frank laughter showed her gums as well as her teeth, and made one wish that her sense of humour were not quite so keen.

"I see you are one of us," she said. "What I call one of the Jolly Fraternity. No, Ohio is still enjoying peace. But—if you follow me—from the States peace will come; there we must fix our hopes. If we can get those millions of brothers and sisters of ours 'across the duck-pond'—as I call it—to see its urgency, peace must come. For brothers and sisters they are, you know; patriotism will come in time to be considered a vice. How can one's soul—if you take my meaning—be affected by the latitude and longitude in which one's body was born? From the States the truth shall come, salvation shall dawn in the west. Listen to me trying to be poetic, it makes me laugh."

One noticed that it did.

"War is so reasonless as to be funny," she said.

"But you haven't told me yet about the little chance that you thought would tickle Olympus," said Kew.

"You're laughing at me," said Mrs. Russell. "But I don't mind, for I laugh at myself. I like you. Shake."

Kew immediately thought her a nice woman, though peculiar.

Mr. Russell looked in and saw the Shake in progress. He murmured something and withdrew hurriedly. For a moment they could hear his agitated voice in the passage reciting Milton to his Hound.

"Do listen to my husband, never silent," said Mrs. Russell. "Did you ever see a man like him?"

There is no real answer to this sort of question, so Kew said "Yo," which is always safe. Then he added, "Do tell me about the little chance."

"This was the little chance," smiled Mrs. Russell. "We ought to have had a tremendously successful peace-meeting in a certain town in Ohio. We had every reason to expect three thousand people, and we thought of proposing the re-naming of the town—calling it Peace. But the little chance was a printer's error—the advertisement gave the date wrong. A crowd turned up at the empty hall, and two days later, when we arrived, they were so tired of us that they booed our demonstration. Just the stupidity of an inky printer between us and success."

"Do you mean to say that but for that we should have had peace by now?" asked Kew in a reverent voice.

"You never know," said Mrs. Russell. "That meeting might have been the match to light the flame of peace all over the world. It's bitterly and satirically funny, isn't it, what Fate will do. Ha-ha-ha."

Cousin Gustus laughed hysterically in chorus, and then said that his head ached, and that he thought he would go to bed early. Anonyma led him away.

"Please don't make peace for a week or two yet," begged Kew. "Let me see what I can do first. I am going tomorrow."

"How foolish of you," said Mrs. Russell. "If you like, I believe I have enough influence to get you to America instead."

"I think I like France best," said Kew. "I don't feel as if I could be content anywhere short of France just now."

"Surely you won't be content anywhere, murdering your fellow-men," said Mrs. Russell. "You won't mind my incurable flippancy, will you? I can't help treating things lightly."

"Not at all," replied Kew. "But I am often content in the intervals of murdering my fellow-men. I play the penny whistle in my dug-out."

"Now tell me," said Mrs. Russell, "what are you all doing here? What mischief are you leading my Herbert into?"

When Kew had recovered from a foolish astonishment at hearing that Mr. Russell was known to others as Herbert, he said, "We're looking—not very seriously—for my sister, who seems to have eloped by herself to the west coast, without leaving us her address."

"I know. Herbert told me that much. A place on the sea-front, isn't it? But you know, I feel a certain responsibility for Herbert, I have neglected him so long. I cannot bear that he should waste his time in what I call these stirring days. You mustn't think because I treat life as one huge joke that I can never be serious. One can wear a gay mask, but—you understand me, don't you? You are one of us."

There was a pause, and then she said, "Ha-ha. Doesn't it seem funny. We've only known each other an hour, and here we are intimate. . ."

Kew obediently allowed himself for a moment to see the humorous side, and then said, "What are your plans then, yours and Mr. Russell's?"

"I have neglected him too long, poor old thing," said Mrs. Russell. "I must stay with him now, and cheer him up. A cheery heart can bridge any gulf, don't you think? You know, I was just what I call a jolly girl when I married him, and afterwards I forgot to grow up, I think.

Perhaps my treatment of him has been rather irresponsible. I must try and make up—what I call 'kiss and be friends,' like two jolly little kiddies."

"Then why not join the motor tour?"

"I would rather take Herbert back to our little nest in London. There's no place like home, as I always say. From there we might work together for the great cause of Peace—what I call 'My Grail.'"

She had crimped hair and a long nose, the tip of which moved when she spoke. You would never have given her credit for such influence as she claimed in the world's affairs. Only her Homeric laughter, and a pair of lorgnettes, reminded you of her greatness.

When Kew finally disentangled himself from the company of this jolly creature, it was very late. But the voice of Anonyma arrested him on his way to bed. Her face, with a corn-coloured plait on each side of it, looked at him cautiously from a dark doorway.

"Kew," said Anonyma, "I won't stand it. We must be rescued."

"Nobody can remove her now without also removing Russ and Christina," said Kew. "The reconciliation has gone too far."

"Then Russ must be sacrificed, and even the car," said Anonyma firmly. "Gustus and I can hire if we must. That woman must be removed. The jealous cat!"

Kew began to see light. "I'll rescue you, then," he replied. "I'll think of a way in my bath."

Next morning a great noise, centring in the bathroom, overflowed through the inn. It was the noise of Kew singing joyful extracts from *Peer Gynt*. Do you remember the beginning of the end of the Hall of the Mountain King? It goes:

> *"Bomp—chink. . . Bomp—chink. . .*
> *Tootle—tootle—tootle—tootle—tootle—tootle-tee. . .*
> *Bomp-chink, . . ."*
> etc., etc.

The way in which Kew rendered this passage, notoriously a difficult one for a solo voice, would have conveyed to any one who knew him that he had solved both his problems.

Anonyma knocked on the bathroom door, and said, "Cousin Gustus's headache is still bad."

Kew therefore broke into Anitra's Dance, which is more subdued.

Before breakfast he and Mr. Russell and the Hound walked to the downs. The motor tour seemed to have come to a standstill. Cousin Gustus's headache could be felt all over the house.

The moment Mr. Russell and Kew were out of earshot of the inn, Kew made such a violent resolve to speak that he nearly broke a tooth.

"Russ," he said, "I want to get off my chest for your benefit something that has been worrying me awfully."

Mr. Russell made no answer. He had got out of the habit of answering.

"It's about Jay," continued Kew. "I must break to you first that Jay's 'house on the sea-front,' with all its accessories—gulls, ghosts, turrets, aeroplanes, and Friends—is one large and elaborate lie. She and I are very much alike. The only difference between us used to be her skirt, and now she has gone a good way towards discarding that. She is nowhere near the sea. She is in London. Now you, Russ, are what she and I used to call an 'Older and Wiser—'"

Mr. Russell jumped violently, but uttered nothing except a little curse to his dog, which was almost under his feet.

"—And you are about the only person I could trust, in my absence, to get Jay out of an uncommonly silly position. I can't bear her present pose. It must stop at once, and if I had time I would stop it myself. I have unfortunately sworn not to give her away to the Family, so I come to you. She is a 'bus-conductor."

Mr. Russell refrained from jumping. I believe he had expected it. But he said, "It would be too funny."

Kew looked at him nervously, fearing for a moment lest Mrs. Russell's sense of humour had proved infectious.

Mr. Russell was thinking how funny it would be if the finger of desirable coincidence had touched his life. How funny if a nice piece of six-shilling fiction should have taken upon itself to make of him its hero. Too funny to be true.

But you, I hope, will remember that the coincidence was not so funny as he thought, since Jay had beckoned to it with her eyes open.

"Now, I have a prejudice against 'bus-conductors," said Kew.

"Why?" asked Mr. Russell rather indignantly.

"I can't explain it. If I could, it wouldn't be a prejudice, it would be an opinion. But—well—just think. . . The trousered 'bus-conductors probably ask her to walk out with them in Victoria Park on Sundays."

"I see your point," said Mr. Russell.

"You are about double as old as she is—if I may say so—and you are not one of the Family, two great advantages. You know, Jay has suffered from not meeting enough Older and Wiser people. She has had to worry out things too much by herself; she has never been talked to by grown-ups whom she could respect. Anonyma never talked with us, though she occasionally 'Had a Good Talk.' She never played, but sometimes suggested 'Having a Good Game.' It's different, somehow. You, Older and Wiser without being too old or too wise, might impress Jay a lot, I think, because you don't say overmuch. And I want you to tell her something of what I feel about it too."

"I never realised before that from your point of view there was any advantage in being Older and Wiser," said Mr. Russell.

"You don't mind my saying all this?" said Kew. It was an assumption rather than a question.

"Not at all. But I don't understand exactly what you want me to do."

"To give up this idiotic motor tour," said Kew. "And go back to London, and talk Jay out of her 'bus-ism. I want her to leave it off, and let the Family discover her romantically enjoying some passable imitation of her Secret World. I want the Family never to know of all that lay between. I do want it all to come right. I'm going off today, and I may not see her again. And I know hardly any trustable person but you."

"Right," said Mr. Russell.

He thought: It's too funny to be true, but if it isn't true, I shall be surprised.

Kew enlarged to him on the details of his mission.

On the breakfast table, when they returned, they found a letter from Jay, evidently written for private circulation in the Family.

Dear Kew

I have just come in from a walk almost as exciting as it was beautiful. We walked through our village, which clings to both sides of a crack-like harbour that might just contain a carefully navigated walnut-shell. The village is grey and white, all its walls are whitewashed, all its roofs are slate with cushions of stone-crop clinging to them. Sea-thistles grow outside its doors, seagulls are its only birds. The slope on which it stands is so steep that the main road is on a level with the roofs on one side, and if you were absentminded, you might walk on to a roof and fall down a chimney before you became aware that you had strayed from the street. But we were not absent-minded. We sang Loud Songs all the way. We ran across the grass after the shadows of the round clouds that bowled across the sky. In single file we followed the dog Trelawney after the seagulls. Everything was so clear that we could see the little rare island that keeps itself to itself on our horizon. I don't know its name; they say it bears a town and a post-office and a parson, but I don't think this is true. I think that island is an intermittent dream of ours. When you get beyond the village, the cliff leaves off indulging in coves and harbours and such frivolities, and decides to look upon itself seriously as a giant wall against a giant sea. Only it occasionally defeats its own object, because it stands up so straight that the sea finds it easier to knock down. On a point of cliff there was a Lorelei seagull standing, with its eye on Trelawney. It had pale eyes, and a red drop on its beak. And Trelawney, being a man-dog, did what the seagull meant him to do. He ran for it, he ran too far, and fell over the edge. Well, this is not a tragic incident, only an exciting one. Trelawney fell on to a ledge about ten foot below the top of the cliff, and sat there in perfect safety, shrieking for help. My Friend said: "This is a case of 'Bite my teeth and Go.'" It is a saying in this family, dating from the Spartan childhood of my Friend, that everything is possible to one who bites his teeth and goes. The less you like it, the harder you bite your teeth, and it certainly helps. My Friend said: "If we never meet again, remember to catch and hang that seagull for wilful murder. It would look rather nice stuffed in the hall." The cliff overhangs rather just there, and when he got over the edge, not being a fly or used to walking upside down, he missed his footing. We heard a yelp from Trelawney. But the seagull's conscience is still free of murder, my Friend only fell on to Trelawney's ledge. So it was all right, and we ate our hard-boiled eggs on the scene of the incident.

"I remember—" said Mr. Russell.
"That letter," said Anonyma, "ought to help us a bit."

She was quite bright, because Kew had conveyed to her the hope that the plot for the rescue of the Family was doing well. Cousin Gustus also, with no traces of a headache except a faint smell of Eau-de-Cologne, had come down hopefully to breakfast.

"Obviously the North coast of Cornwall," said Mrs. Russell. "The village might be Boscastle, and the island is surely Lundy. . . Such an intensely funny name, Lundy, isn't it? Ha-ha! For some reason it amuses me more and more every time I hear it. It reminds me of learning geography with the taste of ink and bitten pen in my mouth. I used to catch my sister's eye—just as I'm catching yours now—and laugh ever so much, over Lundy. I used to be a terror to my governesses."

"I'm very much afraid that I can't spare much more time for the motor tour," said Mr. Russell, and Anonyma was so anxious for the first signs of rescue that she actually let him speak. "Business in London. I dare say I could get you to Cornwall within the next few days, but some time this week I must get back to town."

"I'll come with you," said his wife. "You can't shake me off so easily, my dear. Ha-ha!"

"It's too rainy to start today," said Cousin Gustus. "I have known people drowned by swollen rivers and such while trying to travel in just such a deluge as this. We will start tomorrow."

"Wet or fine," added Anonyma.

"The fact remains," said Kew, "that I must leave you by the ten something. I must leave you to sniff without my help, like bloodhounds, along the trail of the elusive Jay. But I won't bid any one a fervent good-bye, because I daresay I shall be back again on leave for lack of anything else to do in three weeks' time, if we can't get across the Channel. In that case I'll meet you one day next month—say at Land's End or the Firth of Forth. Otherwise—say forty years hence in Heaven."

"It is very wrong to joke about Death," said Cousin Gustus. "I once knew a man who died with just such a joke on his lips."

"I hope it was a better joke than that," said Kew. "It can't be wrong to laugh at Death. Death is such a silly, cynical thing that a little wholesome leg-pulling by an impartial observer ought to do it good."

Mr. Russell was heard asking his Hound in a low voice for the truth about Death and Immortality.

So Kew went away, and left the Family gazing at the rain. Mrs. Russell was conducting a mysterious process known as writing up notes. It was hardly possible, by the way, that Anonyma could have loved the possessor of a rival notebook.

It rained very earnestly. There was no hole in the sky for hope to look through. The puddles in the village street jumped into the air with the force of the rain. You will, without difficulty, remember that it rained several times in the Spring of 1916. But this day was a most perfect example of its kind.

Cousin Gustus was both depressed and depressing. I am afraid I have not given you a very flattering portrait of Cousin Gustus. I ought to have told you that he was very well provided with human affections, and that he loved Kew better than any one else in the world. I might say that the departure of Kew let loose Cousin Gustus's intense grievance against the Germans, except that I could hardly describe a grievance as let loose that had never been pent up.

Cousin Gustus was always angry with the Germans whatever they did, but the thing that made him more angry than ever was to read in his paper some report admitting courageous or gracious behaviour in a German.

"The partings and the troubles that these Germans have caused ought to hang like mill-stones round their necks for ever," said Cousin Gustus. "Talk about Iron Crosses—Pish! I should like to have a German here for ten minutes. I should say to him: 'My Kew was a good boy, I would almost say a clever boy, doing well in his profession: no more thought than that dog has of being a soldier till War broke out. Does that look as if we were prepared for War?' I should say. 'Doesn't that show where the blame lies?' What could he answer?"

Mr. Russell and his Hound were apparently listening, but they could offer no suggestions.

"Kew's going has upset me so that my headache has returned, and I cannot get any Aspirin here," continued Cousin Gustus. "I know a man who was very much addicted to these neuralgic headaches, who committed suicide by throwing himself from the bathroom window, solely owing to neuralgia. And the rain does nothing towards improving matters. They say the German guns bring on the rain. I tell you there is no limit to their guilt. Look at this morning's paper: 'The enemy bombarded this section of our front with increasing intensity during the day. . .' I ask you, Is THAT WAR?"

"Yes," said Mr. Russell absently.

"Nonsense," said Cousin Gustus. "What we ought to do is to shoot every German we can catch. Shooting's too good for them. Hang them. That would teach them. Any Government but ours would have thought of it long ago. Iron Crosses, indeed, Pish!"

Cousin Gustus finds the Iron Cross very useful for the filling up of crannies in his edifice of wrath.

Anonyma said: "When I think of those old fairy-like German songs, I feel as if I had lost a bit of my heart and shall never find it again. That is what I regret most about this War. It is bad art."

"Art, indeed," said Cousin Gustus. "Why, every time they steal a picture they get an Iron Cross. I know a man who saw a German wearing a perfect rosary of Iron Crosses; the fellow was boasting of having bayoneted more babies than any other man in the regiment. Listen to this: 'The enemy attacked the outskirts of the village of What D'you Call'em, and engaged our troops in hand-to-hand fighting.' Think of it, and we used to say they were a civilised race. At the point of the bayonet, it says—isn't it atrocious? 'The enemy were finally repulsed at the point of the bay—' oh well, of course that may be different. I don't pretend to be a military expert. . ."

"I hate the Germans," said Anonyma, "because they have spoilt my own idea of them. I hate having a mistake brought home to me."

"I hate the Germans," began Mr. Russell, "because—"

"I'm going for a walk," said Anonyma. "I am sick of sitting here and hearing you two old fogies argue about the War. If War is bad art, it is vulgar to refer to it."

I know exactly what Mr. Russell was going to say. He had a vague culinary metaphor in his mind. I hate the Germans because they are underdone, they are red meat. Their vices and their virtues and their music, and their greed and their fairyism and their militarism, all seem to have been roasted in a hurry, and to contain, like red meat, the natural juices to an extent that seems to us excessive. The reason why some of us dislike red meat is that it reminds us too much of what our food originally was. As we ourselves, possibly, are rather overcooked by the fire of civilisation, this vulgar deficiency in our enemy is very apparent to us. This is an elaborate, but not a pleasing analogy, and it was fortunate that Mr. Russell was interrupted. Otherwise, I think he might have been trying to this day to explain it to an exasperated Cousin Gustus. He spoke of it to his Hound, and the idea interested that animal very much.

Mr. Russell, unfortunately, had a cold, and was therefore unable on such a wet day to leave the house or Cousin Gustus. But Anonyma went out in a mackintosh that gave her the "silhouette" of a Cossack, and a beautiful little tarpaulin sou'wester, and high boots, and a skirt short enough to give the boots every chance of advertisement. The notebook was safe in a water-tight pocket.

She covered with great speed and enthusiasm the few miles to the sea. She reached it at a point where the cliff dwindled into flatness, where the gentle tide rattled on pebbles instead of on sand, where the tall breakwaters contradicted the line of the shore. The furthest breakwater had seaweed like hair waving on the water. At intervals it would seem to be thrust up between two glassy waves, like a victim beckoning for deliverance from the grip of some monster. And then the sea's lips would close on it again. The sea was freckled by the rain, the waves were beaten into submission. The tide was rather low, and not very far away a great company of porpoises bowed each other through the mazes of a slow quadrille. There were a few rocks spotted like leopards, and on one of these a young brown seagull rested, and allowed itself occasionally to be washed gracefully away.

"Lazy Nature!" said Anonyma reprovingly. "To sketch such a scheme in a few careless lines."

For the whole world was rain-colour. There was no horizon to the sea, the downs were blotted out, the wet shingle reflected its surroundings, the waves broke unmarked by foam or shadow. There was nothing but the porpoises and the breakwaters and the rocks, and a little bald sand dune, sketched on the canvas of that pale day.

Anonyma perpetuated in her notebook her opinion of Nature as an artist. On the whole, it was a flattering opinion. Then she sat on the breakwater, and thought how fortunate she was to be able to think such interesting thoughts about what she saw. How fortunate to enjoy thought and to cause thought! How fortunate to feel oneself a member of the comforting fellowship of intelligence! "It is much more delightful," Anonyma informed the sea, "to be intelligent than to be beautiful. Why do we all try to make our outsides beautiful? There is competition in beauty, but there is brotherhood in intelligence. To be clever is to share a secret and a smile with all clever people." A vision of the coast of the United Kingdom encircled by a ring of consciously clever Anonymas sitting on breakwaters, sharing each with all a secret and a smile, came vaguely to her.

She put all that she could of her soliloquy into her notebook.

And then she noticed the face of a man, with its eyes upon her, appearing stealthily over a breakwater. The face wore the grin that some people wear when they are doing anything with great caution. This gave it a very empty, bright expression, like the mask that represents comedy in a theatre decoration. The face dropped down behind the breakwater, after meeting Anonyma's surprised eye for a second or two.

Anonyma kept her head.

First she thought it was the face of a bather, the path to whose clothes she was unwittingly barring.

Then she thought it was the face of a picnicker, resentful of her intrusion.

Then she thought it was the face of a German spy.

The first two of these three thoughts she rejected because the weather reduced their possibility to a minimum. The third she instinctively adopted as a certainty. The face at once became obviously German in her eyes. It was broader about the chin than about the forehead, it was pink, the architecture of the nose was painfully un-English.

She scanned the sea for the periscope of a submarine.

Anonyma remembered that she had written in her notebook, a day or two before, an intimate description of the coast as seen from the Ring. She also remembered distinctly seeing in the bar of the inn a notice warning her to the effect that walls—and probably breakwaters—have ears and eyes in these days, and that the German Government has a persistent wish to possess itself of private diaries and notebooks.

"I am having an adventure," said Mrs. Gustus. "I must keep cool."

She got up from her breakwater, holding her notebook very tightly, and began to walk away. When she looked back, she saw the top of the man's head moving behind the breakwater, in a parallel direction to her own course. When he reached the point where the breakwater ended and denied him cover, he wavered for a moment, and then, with an expression of elaborate indifference, followed her.

"I must keep even cooler than this," thought Anonyma. "I must try and catch the spy."

She walked across some waste land sown with memories of picnics, and reached the main road. The man crossed the waste land behind her. He tried in a futile way to look as if he were not doing so.

On the main road, Anonyma turned and waited for him. It seemed useless in that empty landscape to sustain the pretence that they were unaware of each other.

"Did you wish to speak to me?" she asked, as well as she could for the great lump of excitement that beat in her throat. Before her eyes visions of headlines danced: "LADY NOVELIST'S PLUCKY CAPTURE OF A SPY."

The man became dark red as she spoke. "Yes," he said. "I wanted to ask you what you were writing in that notebook?"

Anonyma paused for a moment, as she decided what she ought to do. Then she said in a hoarse voice: "I have detailed military information about this coast for twenty miles round in my notebook, with accurate reports as to the depth of the water. If you come to my lodgings in D——, I can show you a map that I have made."

A tremor ran through the stranger.

"A map?" he repeated.

"Yes, a map," said Anonyma; and then, as he did not move, she added on the spur of the moment, "Also a design for a new kind of bomb which I bought from a man in London."

"A bomb?" he said.

Anonyma thought that he was evidently a foreigner, though his accent was English. He seemed to find English rather difficult to understand.

"Why do you tell me all this?" he asked finally.

"Because I recognise your face as that of a sp—I mean a fellow-worker in the great brotherhood of espionage," said Anonyma.

"Come on, then," said the man.

So they walked off together.

"Why did you take up this—calling?" asked the man presently. "Are you a German?"

"Well, more or less," said Anonyma. "At least, I have never been a Christian. I believe that one must take either War or Christianity seriously. Hardly both."

It was a good opportunity for a monologue. Obviously the stranger was not one who would resent a monopoly of the conversation.

"After all, men are only minor gods," said Anonyma, "and War is what gods were born for. Germany knows that. That's why, under the present circumstances, I'd rather take German money than English."

"Are we anywhere near D—— yet?"

Anonyma hoped that he still had no suspicions. His voice was distinctly nervous. To reassure him, she said, "Why did you take up espionage yourself?"

"Why, indeed?" said the stranger in an ardent voice. "Of course the pay was enormous. Twenty thousand francs if I could get an exact chart of the South Coast."

"Why francs?" asked Anonyma.

"Not francs. I find these various currencies so confusing, don't you? Of course I mean pfennigs."

"Twenty thousand pfennigs?" said Anonyma. "Look here, are you trying to be funny?"

"Far from it," said the man. "To tell you the truth, I am awfully nervous."

"Of me?"

"Yes. No. I mean of discovery."

"You don't seem to be absolutely cut out for your job," said Anonyma.

They walked in silence for a while. Anonyma sought through her mind to find something she could say in keeping with her part. She decided finally on a rather ambiguous though imposing attitude.

"The Germans have discovered the truth that anything good is belligerent, love included. You can't fight properly with any weapon but your life. Death is not the only thing that passes by the peace-man. He remains alive, but he also remains ignorant. All peace-men are really women in disguise, and all women are utterly superfluous today. We only know men. People who disapprove of War shall have no part in peace. The peace shall be ours who suffered for it, and only we have earned it. The only decent thing left for the Americans and Quakers to do now is to hold their tongues when peace comes. They haven't earned the right to rejoice."

"I am a Quaker," said the stranger.

"I didn't know the Germans allowed Quakers at large."

"I am not a German," said the stranger.

"Then what has happened?" asked Anonyma, standing suddenly still at the top of the main street of D——. "Why did you want my notebook?"

"Because I could plainly see you taking notes in it."

"You thought me a spy?"

"You don't leave me much room for doubt."

They guided each other to the gate of the police-station. There they stopped again.

"This is where I was bringing you," said Anonyma, as their eyes fell simultaneously on the label over the door: "Sussex County Police."

"It seems to me that honours are easy," she added after a pause. "Don't you see what has happened?"

The stranger thought for a moment with a look of dawning relief on his pink face. "But you couldn't have made up all those dreadful opinions," he said.

"I didn't," said Anonyma. "I meant them all—as applied to England."

"Don't you think we'd better take each other in to make sure?" suggested her companion. "The Inspector's quite a good sort. I know him well. . ."

"You may read my notebook if you like to make quite sure," said Anonyma. "I'm almost sure the Inspector would have either too much or too little sense of humour for the situation."

She was conscious of a certain disappointment. Her adventure had fallen flat, she felt no pleasure in the idea of painting a vivid word-vignette for the people at home. Even her notebook must never hear of this morning's work.

"How foolish of you," she said irritably. "Do I look like a spy?"

"Do I?"

She felt impelled to be angry with him, and seized upon another pretext.

"You are a conscientious objector, I suppose. And what business has a conscientious objector to be spy-hunting? Do I understand that you will only help your country when you can do it vicariously, through the police, with no risk to yourself? It isn't very dignified."

"A spy is outside every pale," said the stranger. "My conscience objects to the shedding of blood. Yet it is an English conscience all the same."

"English?" said Anonyma. "If you won't die for England, England isn't yours to love. You shall not have that honour."

"If dying for England is the test of a patriot," said the pink Quaker, "what about you?"

"I would die for England. I work for England," said Anonyma.

(Four hours a week.)

She went on: "I have told you already that women—in either sex— are superfluous today. But after all, real women were born to their burden, women were born to put up with second bests. And also posterity is mostly a woman's job. But you were born a man, with a great heritage of honour. You have kicked that honour away. You have sold your birthright."

The Quaker was the sort of man in whose face and mind one could see exactly what his mother was like. Some men are like that, and others, one would say, could never have been so intimate with a woman as to be born of her.

"My soul is greater than I am," said the stranger. "There is no command that drowns the command of the soul. I cannot possibly be wrong."

"You could not possibly be right," said Anonyma. "Good-morning."

Anonyma, on her return to the inn, was very generous with "word-vignettes" dealing with Nature. Her Family during supper was not left in ignorance as to the Peace and Meaning of the Sea, and the Parallel between Waves and Generations, and the Miracles of the Mist, and the Tranquil Musing of the Beaches, and the Unseen Imminence of the Downs. "It would make a wonderful background to a short story," said Anonyma, and then she stopped rather abruptly. Her silence after that might have struck the Family as strange, had it not coincided with the arrival of the evening paper, which turned the listeners' thoughts to less beautiful matters.

"Air raid," said Cousin Gustus. "I prophesied quite a long time ago that we should have another raid, but nobody ever listens to what I say. Two horses killed somewhere in the Eastern Counties."

"I thought Somewhere was a town in France, ha-ha," said Mrs. Russell.

"Was London attacked?" asked Mr. Russell. "I'm rather anxious about—St. Paul's. . ."

Anonyma rose to the surface again. "I had such a wonderful talk with a 'bus-conductor once about his experiences during a raid. Such an intelligent man. I dearly love 'bus conductors, such an interesting and vivacious class. I should feel it an honour to be intimate with one. He told me in the most vivid terms how a bomb fell in the street in front of his 'bus, blowing the preceding 'bus to atoms. He told me how his driver turned the 'bus in what he called 'The spice of 'arf a crown,' and plunged into a side street. He said that he could see the Zeppelin balanced on its searchlights like 'a sausage on stilts,' and when it was directly above them, the top of his 'bus was suddenly cleared of people as if by magic, except for one man who put up an umbrella and 'sat tight.' I pitied the conductor, it must have been a terrible experience, his eyes were starting from his head,—bulging like a rabbit's,—he said he had a wife and baby up Leyton way, and that he was so worried about them that he frequently called out his list of destinations the wrong way round."

"Look here," said Mr. Russell, "I think I'd better go up and see about—"

"Nonsense," said his wife. "I refuse to go to London until the moon is there to protect me, as it were. So comic to look upon a heavenly body as a practical protection. I will not allow you to run needlessly into danger. Only this morning you were making plans to go to Cornwall, naughty boy."

"No, but—"

"Darling, I insist," said Mrs. Russell. "Cornwall it is for the present. If you say another word I shall smack you and put you in the corner, ha-ha."

Cornwall it was.

The Family drew near to its destination on a misty day. The sun shone not at all, but occasionally showed its bare pale outline through a veil of cloud. The road in front of Christina was so dim that Mr. Russell could people it for himself with imaginations. Now a knight in armour stood at the next corner, now a phantom sea gleamed over the curve of the road, now he saw great slim ghosts beckoning him on.

There were real sheep every few hundred yards, for a sheep fair was taking place somewhere near by. The sheep came out of the mist like armies of giants, and shrank as they grew clearer. The roads were rippled with the footprints of many sheep. Even when there were no sheep in sight, the mist filled their places with ghostly flocks.

Each sheep as it passed examined the wheels of Christina as long as the dogs allowed it to do so. Each flock was followed by two men, and sometimes a child in ill-fitting clothes on a pony, and sometimes a woman with a shawl over her head.

Anonyma's notebook became very restless, and finally Mr. Russell was obliged to drive the Family to the point whither the sheep were bound.

So they went to the little town, through which the excitement of the fair thrilled like the blast from a trumpet. Bewildered sheep looked in at its shop windows; farmers in dog-carts shouted affectionate remarks to each other across its village green, and introduced dear friends at a great distance to other dear friends with much formality. Dogs argued in a professional way about the merits of their sheep. Mr. Russell's Hound, who had never before heard the suggestion that dogs were intended for any purpose but ornament, looked on breathless with surprise. His morals were affected for life by the revolutionary sight of a dog biting the tail of a disobedient sheep. "I'll try it in Kensington Gardens," thought Mr. Russell's Hound, as he looked nervously at his master.

Christina, the motor-car, found her way to the centre of this activity. There the sheep bleated in tight confinement, and to each pen was attached the appropriate dog, looking very self-conscious. Dogs who had come from great distances to buy sheep were anxiously sniffing up the smell of their purchases, so that no mistake might be made on the way home. Over the line of pens a two-plank viaduct ran, and it was bent continually by the weight of large shepherds balancing their way along to take a bird's-eye view of possible bargains. A facetious auctioneer with the village policeman's arm round his neck was sitting on the wall at the end of the field, addressing everybody very frequently as "Gentlemen." Sheep arrived and sheep departed constantly.

"Isn't it terribly slavish, somehow?" said Anonyma. "The sheep never being consulted at all. Bought and sold and smelt and spat upon as if they had no heart beating beneath that wool. No 'Me,' as Jay used to say."

Mr. Russell heard and remembered. There were few doubts left in him as to the truth of his too-funny miracle.

He had a little tune, the scaffolding of a poem, in his head, and to the sound of it he lived that day, although I don't expect he ever got the poem into words.

If you start your idea along an uncertain course, you have to stop and start afresh to get it straight. You can never finish it when once it has a crooked swing. I gather that motor cyclists occasionally have much the same experience with their machines.

But Mr. Russell, with a mind steering a tangled course, asked for nothing better. He was very nearly sure of romance for the first time in his life.

I hope that the feeling of making poetry is not confined to the people who write it down. There is no luxury like it, and I hope we all share it. I think perhaps the same thrill that goes through Mr. Russell and me when the ghost of a completed thing begins to be seen, also delights the khaki coster who writes his first—and very likely last— love-letter from France; and the little old country mother who lies awake composing the In Memoriam of her son for a local paper; and the burglar "down 'Oxton" who takes off his cap as a child's funeral goes by. The feeling is: "This is a thing out of my heart that I am showing. This is my best confession, and nobody knew there was this within me." I am sure that that great glory of poetry in one's heart does not wait on achievement. If it did, what centuries would die unglorified. It is just perfection appearing, to your equal pride and shame, a perfection that never taunts you with your limitations.

Mr. Russell and Christina knew well their road through the mist that afternoon. There was no difficulty in the world, and no need to see or to think. The sign-posts all spoke the names of fated places. It was useless for Anonyma to study the map, she found no mention there of the enchanted way on which their course was set.

"We will not go through Launceston," said Anonyma. "There must be a quicker way to the sea than that."

Mr. Russell cared not for her and cared not for Launceston. The spell was cast upon Christina's wheels. There was no escaping the appointed way. Launceston reached out its net and caught them. Almost as far as the post office, Anonyma was protesting: "We will Not go through Launceston."

"Launceston was determined to get us," laughed Mrs. Russell. "Ha-ha! isn't it humorous the way things happen?"

The sun was setting as they first saw the Cornish sea. The sky was swept suddenly clear of mist. The seagulls against the sky were like little crucified angels.

The road ran to the shore.

The sun had little delicate clouds across its face, like the islands in a Japanese painting. The wet rocks that lay in the sun's path were plated with gold, and the tall waves with shadowed faces made of that path a ladder. The fields of foam on the sea looked very blue in the pale light.

The sun was like an angel with a flaming sword. The angel dipped his feet into the sea.

The sun was like a flaming stage for the comedies of gods. A ship passed dramatically across it. One's dazzled eyes saw great phantom ships all over the sea.

The sun was like a monster with horns of fire that pierced one's two eyes. And gradually it sank.

The sun was like a word written between the sea and the sky, a word that was swallowed up by the sea before any man had time to read it. There was suddenly no sun. The little forsaken clouds were like flames for a moment, and then they were blown out.

Mr. Russell waved his right hand towards great cliffs like the towers of kings behind the village.

"This is the place," he said.

If I have dared to surrender some imitation of splendour,
Something I knew that was tender, something I loved that was brave,
If in my singing I shewed songs that I heard on my road,
Were they not debts that I owed rather than gifts that I gave?

If certain hours on their climb up the long ladder of time
Turned my confusion to rhyme, drove me to dare an attempt,
If by fair chance I might seem sometimes abreast of my theme,
Was I translating a dream? Was it a dream that you dreamt?

High and miraculous skies bless and astonish my eyes;
All my dead secrets arise, all my dead stories come true.
Here is the Gate to the Sea. Once you unlocked it for me;
Now, since you gave me the key, shall I unlock it for you?

M an ought to feel humble when he reflects upon the fact that he can survive, and even thrive on, any distress except distress of the body. God can wither his soul, and still he lives. Grief can swallow his heart, and still he lives. But his stomach can kill him.

"All is apparently over between me and Peace," thought Jay. "But there must be something to take the place of Peace."

There is only one thing that can adequately usurp the place of Peace. But its name did not occur to Jay.

She did not know what had happened to her. She felt constantly a little mad. Irresponsible wants clamoured in her breast from morning till night, and all night the company of her Secret Friend was more glorious than ever. She ran to her world as you perhaps run to church, yet even there she felt expectant.

When a tall tough thundercloud bends across the sky I watch for the first flash, and listen for the first roar, and in my heart stillness seems impossible and at the same time imperative.

So Jay waited, feeling all the time that she could not wait another minute.

> *You shall not hear whence comes my fear.*
> *You shall not know the name of it.*
> *But out of strife it came to life,*
> *And only striving came of it.*
> *Though for its sake my heart may break,*
> *Yet worse would I endure for it.*
> *This thing shall be a God to me,*
> *I will not seek a cure for it.*

She thought a good deal about Mr. Russell. I am sure that he would have laughed painfully could he have seen the picture of himself that remained with the 'bus-conductor. The picture made him thinner, and his eyes more intelligent, and the line of his mouth happier, but it did not make him look younger, because Jay liked him to be Older and Wiser. He never came into the Secret World; several times she tried to drag him thither, but always at the critical moment he got left outside. Yet I cannot say that in her Secret World she missed him; the point of the bubble enchantment is that there is nothing lacking in it.

'Bus-conducting is a profession that does not engross the mind unduly. The eye and the ear and the hand work by themselves. Charing

Cross whispered in a conductor's ear at the Bank produces a white ticket from her hand without any calculation on her part. She becomes a penny-in-the-slot machine, with her human brain free for other matters. She grows a great hatred for all fares above fourpence, because they need special thought.

Jay filled her day with unsatisfactory thinking. She found to her surprise that one may love life and yet also think lovingly of death. To live is most interesting in an uneasy way, but to die is to forget at once all these trivial turbulences, to forget equally the people you have loved and the people you have hated, to forget everything you ever knew, to be alone, and to be no longer disturbed by unceasing voices.

At this time I think Jay felt more hatred of everybody than love of any one person. But then, of course, she had vowed to Chloris after the affair with young William Morgan that she would never fall in love again. She said, "I have been through love. It is not a sea, as people say. It is only a river, and I have waded through it."

"Yet there is certainly something very remarkable about that man," she thought. "I don't believe I like him much, I don't want to know him better, though I should like him to know me. I believe he is my real next of kin. I believe he has a Secret World too."

She was on her last homeward journey, and it was one of her early days. The hours of a conductor move up and down the day. Sometimes Jay punctured her first ticket at a time when you and I are asleep, and when the coster-barrows, waving with ferns and fuchsias, move up the Strand like Birnam Wood moving to Dunsinane. On those days she was due home at half-past four or so. On other days she was able to have a late breakfast and to darn her stockings after it, but that meant that she did not get home till very late. Some 'buses, I gather, are called "single 'buses," but in this case the word does not imply celibacy alone. The single 'bus is occupied by one conductor all day long for a fortnight. The "double 'bus" is shared by two conductors, one presiding in the morning and the other in the afternoon. The double state also lasts a fortnight; it is arranged as an opportunity for lady 'bus-conductors to recuperate after the rigours (the more remunerative rigours) of service on a single 'bus. These statements of mine are open to extensive correction. Jay's hours always struck me as so very confusing that it is unlikely I should be able to retail the information correctly. However, it doesn't matter very much.

This was one of the early days on a double 'bus, and Jay was on her last journey, with several restless waking hours between her and possible sleep. Her 'bus was full, but not pressed down and running over. For the moment everybody in it was provided with a ticket. Jay was laboriously thinking small thoughts because she was tired of thinking of Love and Life and other things with capital letters.

She thought of the various indignities to which the public submits its 'bus-tickets. Some people use the ticket as a toothpick, some put spectacles on and read it without understanding, some decorate outstanding features of the 'bus with it. But I myself tear it gradually into small strips, and grind the strips by means of massage into fine powder. If the inspector comes, I am perfectly willing to pour the powder into his hand, and yet he often seems annoyed.

Jay reviewed the perspective of faces that lined her 'bus. They were all ugly, and not one of them was eager. The British public as a whole considers a deaf, dumb, and blind expression the only decent one to wear in a public conveyance. We roar through a wonderful and exciting world, and all the while we sit with glazed eyes and cotton-wool in our ears, and think about ourselves. They were mostly men in Jay's 'bus at that moment; they were almost all alike, and all insignificant, but not one of them knew it. Such a lot of men could never be loved by women, only found expedient.

But there was a sailor, a simple sub-lieutenant, sitting by the door. Sailors are a race apart. They have twisty faces, their boots and gloves look curiously accidental. In London they are rarely seen without a *London Mail* or a *London Opinion* in their grasp. There is something about a sailor that conduces to sentiment in every passer-by, and Jay, who was fleeing from that very feeling, looked hastily at some one else. Her seeking eye lit on a lady who had a complete skunk climbing up the nape of her neck, and a hat of the approximate size of a five-shilling piece worn over her right eyebrow. She looked such a fool that Jay concluded that the look was intentional, and indeed I suppose it must be, for the worst insult you can offer to young ladies of this type is to suggest that they have brains. Jay pondered on this, and then turned elsewhere for inspiration. All roads of thought at that time led to one destination, so she only allowed herself to go a little way along each road.

And presently she reached the end of her journey. She walked home, and Chloris was as usual waiting for her just outside the rocking-horse factory at the corner. Jay, as she passed that factory every day, watched with interest the progress of the grey ghost rocking-horses, eyeless, maneless, and tailless, as they ripened hourly into a form more like that of the friend of youth.

She smelt the little smell that is always astray in Mabel Place, she heard outside in the damp afternoon two rival barrow-men howling a cry that sounded like "One pound hoo-ray!" A neighbour in the garden was exchanging repartee with a gentleman caller. "Biby, siy Naughty Man, Biby, tell 'im what a caution 'e is." But there seemed little hope that the baby would. These sounds were provided with the constant Brown Borough background of shouts and quarrels and laughter and children crying and innumerable noises of work.

"Something has happened," said Jay to Chloris, as they went in. "I feel as if I had no friends tonight. Not even a Secret Friend."

Chloris lay on her lap in her usual attitude, bent into a circle like a tinned tongue. Chloris knew it was no use worrying about these things.

"Funny," thought Jay. "King David was a healthy man of ruddy countenance, and presumably he never lived in the Brown Borough, yet he knew very well what it feels like to have a temperature, and a sore heart, and to be alone in lodgings. Whenever I am very tired, it is funny how my heart quotes those tired Psalms of his, without my brain remembering the words. I wonder how David knew."

The little house was empty but for her. I ought perhaps to have told you before that Nana had been taken ill a month or so ago, and had gone away at Jay's expense to a South Coast Home.

"I'll go round and see Mrs. 'Ero Edwards," said Jay, when she had changed into mufti. "Neither Chloris nor David is adequate to the moment."

The ground-floor back room of Mrs. 'Ero Edwards was crowded. The Chap from the Top Floor was there, and Mrs. Dusty Morgan, and little Mrs. Love from Tann Street, and Mrs. 'Ero Edwards's daughter, Queenie, and several people's children. Conversation never wavered as Jay knocked and came in. When you find that your entrance no longer fills a Brown Borough room with sudden silence, you may be glad and know that you have ceased to be a lidy or a toff.

The Chap from the Top Floor was talking, and everybody else was there to hear him do it, except Mrs. 'Ero Edwards who could hardly bear it, because she only liked listening to herself. Jay sat modestly in a corner and listened, like the other representatives of her generation.

The Chap from the Top Floor was an Older and Wiser Man. His wife could not live with him, but he was very kind and fatherly to every one else, and Jay was rather fond of him. He was about fifty, and anything but beautiful. Also the C.O.S. would not have admired him. But I believe he did a good deal of thinking inside that bristly head of his.

"Ow my dear," said Mrs. 'Ero Edwards, laying a fat hand on Jay's knee. "We're all so 'appy. Dusty's wrote to siy 'e's got the sack from the Army becos of 'is rheumatics. We're 'avin' a bit of a beano becos of it."

Everybody smiled at Jay, and her heart grew warmer. Some one handed her a cup of tea sweetened with half an inch of sugar at the bottom of the cup. The spoon had been plunged to its hilt in condensed milk. What vulgar tastes she had!

"You can never mike a pal of a woman," said the Chap from the Top Floor, continuing an argument for the benefit of an audience of women. "One feller an' another—well—a pal's a pal. But women are all either wives or—, there ain't no manner of palliness in them."

"'Tain't gentlemanly to talk so, Elbert," said Mrs. 'Ero Edwards. "Yore mother was a woman, an' from 'er comes all you know, I'm thinkin', an' all you are. Women is pals with women, an' men is pals with men. It's only when men an' women gets assorted-like that palliness drops out."

"'Usbinds an' wives can be pals," said Mrs. Dusty. "Me an' Dusty useter 'ave a drop an' a jaw together every night for three months after we married. Never 'ad a thought apart, we didn't."

"If I ars't Dusty," said the Top Floor Chap, "I don't know but what 'e wouldn't tell a different tile."

"'Ere, 'bus-conductor, you can talk, an' you're a suffragette," said Mrs. Dusty. "Ain't bein' a pal just as much a woman's job as a man's?"

"What is bein' a pal?" asked Mrs. Love bitterly. "'Avin' some one 'oo drinks wiv you until she's sick, and then blacks your eye for you. There ain't no pals, men or women."

"I think they're rare," said Jay. "Isn't being a pal just refusing to admit a limit? Some people draw the line at a murderer, and some at a suffragette, and some at a vegetarian, and some at a lady who wears the same dress Sundays and week-days, but a real pal draws no line. Women and dogs as well as men can be faithful beyond limit, I think, but it's very rare in anybody."

"'Bus-conductors don't know nothink," said the Chap from the Top Floor in a loud belligerent voice, illuminated by an amiable smile. "I orfen look at 'bus-conductors, an' think, 'Pore devils, they don't know 'arf of life, not even a quarter. They only meets the harisocracy wot 'as pennies to frow about, they never passes the time of day with a plain walkin' feller like me wot ses 'is mind an' never puts on no frills. 'Bus-conducting oughter be done by belted earls an' suchlike, it ain't a real man's job. Pore devils,' I ses, lookin' at 'em bouncin' along, doin' the pretty to all the nobs, wivout so much as puttin' their toe in the mud. 'Pore devils.'"

"'Ere Elbert, 'old your jaw," said the tactful Mrs. 'Ero Edwards, nervous lest Jay should resent this insult to her calling. "Let's all go roun' to the Cross'n Beetle, an' see whether that won't stop 'is noise."

"After all, it's Dusty's birfdiy," said Mrs. Dusty with alacrity.

The day was evidently growing in importance every minute.

"You come along too," said little Mrs. Love, suddenly putting her hand in Jay's.

"No treatin' nowadiys," said the Top Floor Chap amiably. "But I don't mind 'andin' around the price of a drink before we start."

He only extended half-hearted generosity to Jay, because she was, after all, a 'bus-conductor, and to that extent a nob. She shook her head and laughed, when he held out to her the Law-circumventing coin.

Mrs. 'Ero Edwards only really found scope for her voice out of doors. No sooner was she in the street than she seized the arm of the Chap from the Top Floor and shouted him down, as she led him towards the Cross'n Beetle.

Mrs. Dusty and young Queenie walked arm in arm behind them, and whenever they saw a soldier they squeaked loudly, and addressed him invariably as "Colonel Mawmajuke."

Jay and little Mrs. Love, both rather confused and unhappy people, walked hand in hand a little way behind.

"We needn't go as fur as the Cross'n Beetle, if we don't like," said Mrs. Love. "They'll never notice if we 'ook it."

"I don't want to 'ook it," said Jay. "I want to keep very busy listening to noisy people. I don't want to hear myself think."

"You're mopey, eh?" asked Mrs. Love gently.

"I'm cold," said Jay. "I believe I've lost something. I believe I've lost a friend of mine."

"Friends is always gettin' lost," said Mrs. Love. "I told you so. Let's go an' 'ave a look at the pictures. They've got the 'Curse of a Crook' on up the street. Fairly mike yer 'air curl."

"I want noise," said Jay, "a much louder noise than that old piano. The pictures are so horribly quiet. Just an underfed man turning a handle, and an underfed woman hitting an underfed piano. At a play you can at least pretend that the actors are having a little fun too, but the pictures—there's only two sad people without smiles at the bottom of it all. I won't go to the pictures, I'll go and get drunk."

"Come on then," said Mrs. Love. "You won't find no lost friends there, but come on. I'll be yer pal for tonight. You've been a pal to me before now. We're temp'ary pals right enough, there' ain't no permanent kind. You won't find no shivers straying around in the ole Cross'n Beetle. Let's 'urry, an' get drunk, and keep 'and in 'and all the time. That's wot pals oughter do."

Jay suddenly saw the whole world as a thing running away from its thoughts. The crowd that filled the pavement was fugitive, and every man felt the hot breath of fear on the back of his neck. One only used one's voice for the drowning of one's thoughts; one only used one's feet for running away. The whole world was in flight along the endless streets, and the lucky ones were in trams and donkey carts that they might flee the faster.

"Hurry, hurry," said Jay. And she and little Mrs. Love ran hand in hand.

The Chap from the Top Floor and Mrs. 'Ero Edwards were already leading society in the Cross'n Beetle when Jay and Mrs. Love reached it. The barman knew Mrs. Edwards too well to think that she was drunk already, but you or I, transported suddenly thither, would have supposed that her beano was over instead of yet to come.

"'Elbert," said Mrs. 'Ero Edwards, "yo're an 'Un, yo're an internal alien, thet's what's the metter with you. I wonder I 'aven't blacked yer eye for you many a time and oft."

There was almost enough noise even for Jay, and she and Mrs. Love, each armed with a generously topped glass, sat in the background, on the shiny seat that lined the wall.

To Jay this evening was an experiment, an experiment born of weariness of a well-worn road. She watched Mrs. Love blow some of the superfluous froth on to the floor, and did likewise. Directly she had put her lips to the thick brim of her glass she knew that here was the stuff of which certain dreams are made.

She had, I suppose, the weakest head in the world, and in three minutes she was giddy and much comforted. The noise seemed to clothe itself in a veil of music, there was hope in the shining brightness that shone from the bar. The placards that looked like texts and were advertisements of various drinks, seemed like jokes to Jay.

"There are only dreams," she thought very lucidly, "to keep our souls alive. We are lucky if we get good dreams. We'll never get anything better."

Through the glass between the patriotic posters that darkened the windows she could see the morbid colour of London air.

"Apart from dreams," thought this busconducting Omar Khayyám, "there is nothing but disappointment. We expected too much. We expected satisfaction. There is nothing in the world but second bests, but dreams are an excellent second best. Our last attitude must be 'How interesting, but how very far from what I wanted. . .'"

The speed of time, and the hurry of life suddenly rushed upon her again.

"I must hurry," she said. "Or I shan't have lived before I die. I must hurry."

"No 'urry, Jine," said Mrs. Love. "Let's keep in the light for a bit."

"Is this the only light left us, after a deluge of War?" thought Jay. "It doesn't matter, because of course War is hurrying too. Rushing over our heads like the sea over drowned sailors. But it will be over in a minute; this new kind of death must be a temporary death for temporary soldiers. What do fifty years without friends matter? You can hardly breathe before they're done."

She was dazzled and deafened. She had emptied her glass, and she did not know what steps she took to fill it again. Only she found it was suddenly full.

And in a minute she was on the path to the House by the Sea. She had come by a new way.

There was less colour than usual about the sea, a certain air of guilt seemed to haunt the path. And it was extraordinarily lonely, there seemed to be no promise of a Friend waiting at the other end of the path.

She sang the Loud Song to encourage herself, but she did not sing it very loudly.

There is no dream like my dream,
Even in Heaven.
There is no Friend like my Friend,
Even in Heaven.
There is no life like my life,
Even in Heaven.

A voice said, "For 'eaven's sike, Jine, don't begin to sing."

Jay laughed. "Treating me as if I were drunk. . ." she thought. She did not feel giddy any more. She could see the familiar outline of the House against an unpretentious sky, and that calm shape steadied her.

No breath of sound came from the House. The sky was grey, the sea was grey, there was no hint of sunlight. As Jay came to the door she noticed that the honeysuckle in the bowl at the hall window was still there, but dead. The wind had strewn the doorstep with leaves and straws and twigs, little refugees of the air.

In the hall there was an old woman, dressed in a black dress patterned with big red flowers. She was knitting. Her stiff skirts spread out in angular folds round her. Jay knew she was a fellow-ghost, because their eyes met.

Jay felt swallowed up by the silence. She could not speak, even to think, she felt, would be too noisy. The stiff skirt of the old lady made no rustle, the knitting needles made no click. But Jay could see that she was counting. The House seemed to be full of unmoving time. Outside the rain began to fall, and that grey sound enclosed the silence of the House.

After a very long time Jay spoke. "Where is my Friend?" she asked.

"Gone to the War," answered the old woman.

"There is no War in this world," said Jay.

"On the contrary," the fellow-ghost replied, "war is, even here, where Time is not. War is like air, in every house, in every land, on every sea. For ever."

Between her sentences she counted. Unpausing numbers moved her lips.

"On these shores," she said, "time and Life and the sea go up and down. Eternity has no logic. There are no reasons, there is no explanation. But there is always War. There are fighting sea men in the caves on the beach. Haven't you seen them, the dark sea people? Haven't you heard their high voices that were tuned to cut through the voice of the sea? Haven't you found their very wide, long-toed footprints in the sand? Have you walked blind through this world?"

"No," said Jay, "I remember. The women decorate their hair with seaweed, pink and green. I have watched them catch fish with their hands. I have watched them put their babies to play in the pools among the rocks. . ."

"On the cliffs," said the fellow-ghost, "men clad in armour share the camps of the Englishmen who fought at Cressy, and at Waterloo, and at the Marne. On these seas the most ancient pirates sing and laugh in chorus with Nelson's drowned sailors, and with men from the North Sea, men whose mothers still cry in the night for them. Did you think there was any seniority in Eternity?"

"But I don't understand," said Jay. "Time seems to leave itself behind so quickly. . ."

"There is nothing to understand," said the old woman. "There is no explanation. Time does not move. Men move." The noise of the rain seemed to wash out everything but remembrance, and there was no feeling in Jay but a terrible longing to have her Secret Friend with her again, and that long secret childhood of theirs, and to wipe out half her days and all her knowledge, and to hear once more those songs upon the sands of the cove, and to feel the tingling ground of the sunny hills.

"My Friend has never forsaken me before," she said.

She felt a hand press her hand, and she met the eyes of little Mrs. Love.

"Yo're a mousey sort of kid," said Mrs. Love, "sittin' there as if you was in church. Shall we go 'ome? The rine's gettin' worse an' worse, an' it's no good wytin'. I'll see you 'ome."

When Jay, very wet and dazed, reached Eighteen Mabel Place, she found a card pushed under the door. The name on it was Mr. Herbert Russell's, and there was a suggestion in a beautiful little handwriting on the back of it that she should ring him up next morning and tell him when to come and see her, as he had a message from her brother.

"This is the sort of thing that couldn't possibly happen in real life," said Jay. "I must be drunk after all. On no doorstep except Heaven's could one find a message so romantic."

She was instinctively disobedient to Older and Wiser people. She never entertained the idea of telephoning. She could imagine Mr. Russell answering the telephone in a prosaic voice like a double bass. She wrote the following letter:

DEAR SIR

Don't you remember, I was to meet you anyway on the steps of St. Paul's at ten o'clock next Sunday? I will wait till then for the message.

Yours faithfully,
JANE ELIZABETH MARTIN, 'Bus-conductor

"That letter ought to put two and two together for him," she thought, "if he hasn't done it already. It's a complicated little sum, and the result is—what?"

She felt hot and feverish when she wrote the letter. And directly she had posted it she regretted having done so.

"I forget what I wrote," she said. "It is dangerous to post letters to Older and Wiser Men when drunk."

All that night she lay awake and mourned the desertion of her Secret Friend.

You promised War and Thunder and Romance.
You promised true, but we were very blind,
And very young, and in our ignorance
We never called to mind
That truth is seldom kind.

You promised love, immortal as a star.
You promised true, yet how the truth can lie!
For now we grope for hands where no hands are,
And, deathless, still we cry,
Nor hope for a reply.

You promised harvest and a perfect yield.
You promised true, for on the harvest morn,
Behold a reaper strode across the field,
And man of woman born
Was gathered in as corn.

You promised honour and ordeal by flame.
You promised true. In joy we trembled lest
We should be found unworthy when it came;
But—oh—we never guessed
The fury of the test.

You promised friends and songs and festivals.
You promised true. Our friends, who still are young,
Assemble for their feasting in those halls
Where speaks no human tongue.
And thus our songs are sung.

I have very rarely found Sunday in London a successful day. I hate idleness without peace, and festivity without beauty, and noise without music. I hate to see London people in unnatural clothes. I hate to see a city holding its breath.

Jay waited ten minutes on the steps of St. Paul's for Mr. Russell. This was not because he was late, but because she was early; and this again was not because she was indecently eager, but because she had hit on an unexpectedly non-stop 'bus. She felt a fool for ten minutes. And when you have waited ten minutes on those enormous steps under the eye of the pigeons, you will know why she felt a fool.

Mr. Russell arrived in Christina the motor car, and simultaneously a shower fell. From the first moment Jay felt unsuccess in the air of that much-anticipated day. She was introduced to Christina, and said, "But we can't take that thing into the Cathedral."

"We don't want to," said Mr. Russell, although, as he was a born driver, the challenge made him instinctively measure with his eye the depth of the steps, and the width of the doorway, from Christina's point of view. "We don't want to pray. We want to talk."

Anonyma would have been astonished to hear him say this.

"As a matter of fact," said Jay, "I brought Chloris for the same reason."

Chloris was eating the bread which a kind but short-sighted old lady believed herself to be giving to the pigeons.

Mr. Russell had hardly been able to imagine his 'bus-conductor in any dress but that of her calling. Now that he saw her in unambitious London-coloured things, he was glad to notice that her clothes were not Sunday clothes, but the sort that you forget about directly you look away from them.

This was the sort of day that breaks up delusions, and as Christina the motor car started away, Jay discovered that her hat was not adequately attached to her head. There are few discoveries more depressing than this at the beginning of a day of movement.

The bells of St. Paul's began to sing. Little fairy bells dodged behind and about the great notes. But Christina soon swept the sound into the forgotten air behind her.

"I've got a lot to talk to you about," said Mr. Russell as he headed Christina Hackney-way. He was conscious that he was taking his miracle curiously for granted. I don't think he really believed in it yet. For Mr. Russell all truth was haunted by the ghost of a clanking lie. He discerned deceit on the part of Providence where no deceit was. "I'll give you your brother's message first, because it interests me personally least. He is gone. There was a sudden move across the Channel last week, and he went—I suppose—ten days ago now. The message he hadn't time to give you was an appeal to give up 'bus-conducting. He had an absurd idea that you walked out with men-conductors in Victoria Park."

"Not at all absurd," said Jay. "Not half so absurd as the idea of driving out with a casual fare. I know some delightful conductors and drivers; we joke together when the traffic sticks. There is one perfect darling called Edward; his only fault is that he drives a mere Steamer. But we always bow, and once when a horse fell down and we got hung up for twenty minutes in the Strand, he sang me a little song about a star."

Mr. Russell listened to all this very attentively, and then continued: "Your brother wants you to go back to your Family. His last words to me about it were that if you could manage to be ladylike for three years or the duration of War, at the end of that time he and you would go and live by your two selves in New Zealand, and if you liked you need wear no skirts at all there, but riding breeches all the time."

"Ladylike!" snorted Jay. "What's the use of lady-liquity even for five minutes? So Kew sent you as an antidote? I suppose he didn't know you were one of my fares?"

"A fare," said Mr. Russell sententiously, "may, I suppose, be a wonderful revelation, because you only see your fare's eyes for a second, and the things you may see have no limit, and you never know the silly little truth about him. Yet even so, there is more than a ticket and a look between you and me, and you know it."

"Possibly there is a Secret World between you and me," said Jay. "But that's a pretty big thing to divide us."

"Supposing it doesn't divide us?" said Mr. Russell, looking fiercely at the road in front of him. "Supposing it showed me how much I love you?"

"How disappointing!" said Jay in the worst of possible taste. (She was like that today.) "You're ceasing to be an Older and Wiser, and trying to become an ordinary Nearah and Dearah."

("Oh, curse," she thought in brackets. "I shall kick myself tonight.")

"That's a horrid thing to say," said Mr. Russell. "But still I do love you."

"It sounds very Victorian and nice," said Jay, wondering if he could still see her through her veil of bad temper. "But, you know, in spite of

Secret Worlds, and secret souls, and centuries of secret knowledge, we still have to keep up this 1916 farce, and leave something of ourselves in sensible London. How do I know you're not married?"

Mr. Russell thought for a very long time indeed, and then said, "I am."

Jay was not very well brought up. She did not stop the car and step out with dignity into respectable Hackney. She was just silent for a long time.

"As you were," she said to herself, when she found herself able to think again. "This is a bad day, but it will be over in something less than a hundred years."

"You drive well," she said presently, looking with relief from Mr. Russell's face to his hands. Christina the motor car and two 'buses were just then indulging in a figure like the opening steps of the Grand Chain. "You drive as though driving were poetry and every mile a verse."

"After all," she told herself, "the man loves me, and I must at least take an intelligent interest in him."

"Are you a poet?" she added.

Nobody had ever asked Mr. Russell this question before, and not knowing the answer to it, he did not answer.

"I have never written a line of poetry," said Jay. "Or rather, I have several times written a line, but never another line to fit it. Yet because I have a Friend,—I know in what curious and extended order the verses come, and how the tunes come first, and the various voices next, and the words last, and how a good rhyme warms you like a fire, and how the tunes fall away when the thing is finished, and how ready-made it all is really, and yet how tired you feel. . ."

To Mr. Russell it all seemed true, and part of the miracle. He had nothing to add, and therefore added nothing.

"Obviously you are a poet," said Jay. "You have a poetic look."

"What look is that?" asked Mr. Russell, much pleased. It was twenty years since he had even remembered that he possessed a look of his own.

"A silly sullen look," said Jay. Presently she added: "But it must have been disappointing to find yourself a poet in Victorian times. I always think of you Olders and Wisers as coming out of your stuffy nineteenth century into our nice new age with a sigh of relief."

"Oh no," said Mr. Russell. "You must remember that when we were born into it, it became our nice new age, and therefore to us there is no age like it."

"It seems incredible," said Jay. "Did Older and Wiser people ever live violently, ever work—work hard—until their brains were blind and they cried because they were so tired? Did they ever get drowned in seas full of foaming ambitions? Did they ever fight without dignity but with joy for a cause? Did they ever shout and jump with joy in their pyjamas in the moonlight? Did they ever feel just drunk with being young, and in at the start? And were Older and Wiser people's jokes ever funny?"

"We were fools often," said Mr. Russell. "Once, when I was fifteen, I bit my hand—and here is the scar—because I thought I had found a new thing in life, and I thought I was the first discoverer. But as to jokes, you are on very dangerous ground there. One's sense of humour is a more tender point than one's heart, especially an Older and Wiser sense of humour. You know, we think the jokes of your nice new age not half so funny as ours. But as neither you nor I make jokes, that obstacle need not come between us."

"Oh, I think difference of date is never in itself an obstacle," said Jay. "Time is not important enough to be an obstacle."

"You and I know that," said Mr. Russell.

A little unnoticed knot of Salvationists surprised Jay at a distance by singing the tune of a sentimental song popular five years ago, and then they surprised her again, as she passed them, and heard the words to which the tune was being sung. Brimstone had usurped the place of the roses in that song, and the love left in it was not apparently the kind of love that Hackney understands.

"Why don't they sing the old hymn tunes?" asked Jay. "Or tunes like 'Abide with Me'—not very old or very good, but worn down with devotion like the steps of an old church? Why do they take the drama out of it all?"

Chloris at that moment introduced drama into the drive by jumping out of the back seat of Christina. I must, I suppose, admit that Chloris was not Really Quite a Lady. On the contrary, motor 'buses were the only motors she knew. She mistook the estimable Christina for a deformed motor 'bus, and when she smelt Victoria Park, she jumped out. Even for Chloris this was an unsuccessful day. A flash of yelping lightning caught the tail of Jay's eye, and she looked round to see her dignified dog, upside down, skid violently down a steep place into the gutter, and there disappear beneath the skirt of a female stranger who was poised upon the kerb. Unhurt, but probably blushing furiously beneath her fur over her own vulgarity, Chloris was retrieved, and spent the rest of the drive in wiping all traces of the accident off her ribs on to the cushions of Christina. I am glad that Mr. Russell's Hound was not there to witness poor Chloris's unsophisticated confession of caste.

"Where are we going?" asked Jay, when she was calm again.

"God knows where. . ." said Mr. Russell.

"I'm always coming across districts of that name," said Jay severely. "I often direct my enquiring fares to the region of God Knows Where. It is most unsatisfying. Where are we going?"

"On for ever," said Mr. Russell. "Out of the world. To the House by the Sea."

"Then will you please set me down at Baker's Arms?" said Jay. "Do you know, by the way, that Anonyma always says 'Stay' to a 'bus, if she remembers in time not to say 'Hi, stop,' like a common person."

She was talking desperately against failure, but it seemed a doomed day, and nothing she could think of seemed worth saying.

"I want to talk to you about your House by the Sea," said Mr. Russell. "You know I found it."

"Don't tell me any facts," implored Jay. "Don't tell me you pressed half a crown into the palm of the oldest and wisest inhabitant, and found out facts about some nasty young man who was born in seventeen something, and lived in a place called Atlantic View, and wore curls and a choky stock, and fought at Waterloo, and lies in the village church under a stone monstrosity. Don't tell me facts, because I know they will bar me for ever out of my House by the Sea. Facts are contraband there."

"There is no House by that Sea now," said Mr. Russell. "A slate quarry has devoured the headland on which it used to stand. Where the House used to be there is air now. I daresay the ghosts you knew still trace out the shape of the House in the air."

"The ghosts I know," corrected Jay. "Don't put it in the past."

"It's all in the past," said Mr. Russell. "It's all a dream, and an echo, and the ghost of the day before yesterday."

"How do you know?" asked Jay. "How can you tell it's not 1916 that's the ghost?"

She had been taught by her Friend to take very few things for granted, and time least of all.

"I asked you to tell me no facts," she added.

"I'll only tell you two," persisted Mr. Russell. "One is that they have in the church near the quarry a dark wooden figure of a saint, with the raised arm broken, and straight draperies. I saw it, and they told me what I knew already, that it came out of the hall of a house that was drowned in the sea. The other fact is a story that the tobacconist told me, about a wriggly ladder, and stone balls, and the Law. In the tobacconist's childhood they found the stone balls at the foot of the cliff in the sand. That story, too, I knew already. Quite apart from your letters, you little secret friend, I knew the face of that sea directly I saw it."

"But how did you know? How dared you know?"

"Oh well," said Mr. Russell, "you asked me to tell you no facts."

Mr. Russell was not observant. He was not sufficiently alive to be observant. He was much occupied in remembering phantom yesterdays, and I do not think he listened very much to what the 'bus-conductor said. He only enjoyed the sound of her voice, which he remembered. So he did not know that she was unhappy.

They came presently to a separate part of the forest, which is impaled upon a straight white road. The earth beneath the trees was caught in a mesh of shadows. The trees are high and vaulted there, but the forest is very reticent. The detail of its making is so small that you can only see it if you lie down on your face. Do this and you can see the green threads of the earth's material woven across the skeletons of last year's leaves. You can see the little lawns of moss and weeds, too small to name, that make the way brilliant for the ants. You can watch the heroic armoured beetles defying their world. You can cover with a leaf the great open-air public meeting-places of six-legged things. You can see the spiders at work on their silver cranes, you can watch the bold elevated activities of the caterpillars. You can feel the scattered grasses stroke your eyelids, you can hear the low songs of fairies among the roots of the trees. All these things you may enjoy if you lie down, but the forest does not show them to you. The forest pays you the great compliment of ignoring you, and it does not care whether you see its intimate possessions or not. I think perhaps no day is really unsuccessful that gives you forest earth against your forehead, and forest grass between your fingers, and high forest trees to stand between you and the ultimate confession of failure.

Jay and Mr. Russell boarded out Christina the motor car for the day at an inn, and then they sat and gradually introduced themselves to the forest. Showers fell on their hatless heads, and they did not notice. A mole rose like a submarine from the waves of the forest earth, and they did not notice. The butterflies danced like little tunes in the sunlit clearing, and they did not notice. And from a long way off, near the swings, holiday shrieks trailed along the wind, and they did not notice.

Jay told Mr. Russell, one by one, small unmattering things that she remembered out of her Secret World, and each time when she had told him he wondered with regret why he had not remembered it by himself. He had never thought it worth while to remember before; his imagination was crippled, and needed crutches. He had not thought it worth while to think much about the time when he was young, the time when his past had been as big and shining as his future. The longer we live, it seems, the less we remember, and no men and few women normally possess a secret story after thirty. It would not matter so much if you only lost your story, a worse fate than loss befalls it—you laugh at it. It is curious how the world draws in as one gets older and wiser. The past catches one up, the future burns away like a candle. I used to think that growing up was like walking from one end of a meadow to the other, I thought that the meadow would remain, and one had only to turn one's head to see it all again. But now I know that growing up is like going through a door into a little room, and the door shuts behind one.

I think Mr. Russell's point of difference from most older and wiser people was that he had not forgotten the excitement of writing down snatches of his secret story as it came to him, and the passion of tearing up the thing that he wrote, and the delight of finding that he could not tear it out of his heart. He was a silent person, and a rather neglected person, and unbusinesslike, and unsuccessful, and uncultured, and unsociable, and unbeautiful. So there was nothing worse than emptiness where his secret story used to be. He had not found it worth while to fill the space. He had not found it worth while to shut the door.

"Do you remember that Christmas," said Jay, "when there was a blizzard, and a great sea, and the foam blinded the western windows of the House, and the children went out to sing 'Love and joy come to you'? (Those aren't real words any more now, are they? only pretty caricatures.) And when the children came in with snow and foam plastered up their windward sides, do you remember that one of them said, 'Is this what Lot's wife felt like?'"

"I can just remember Love and Joy mixed up with the wind at the window," said Mr. Russell. "But always best of all I can remember the way you looked on. . ."

"Me?" said Jay. "I wasn't there."

"Oh yes you were, and that's what you forget. You were there always, and when I was looking for the House I believe it was always you I was expecting to find there."

"Me! Me, with this same old face?" gasped Jay. "Oh, excuse me, but you lie. You never recognised me in my 'bus."

"I knew without knowing I knew. I remembered without remembering that I remembered. We haven't made a psychical discovery, Jay, we have done nothing to write a book about. Only you remember so well that you have reminded me."

"I don't believe that can be true," said Jay. "I know I wasn't there."

"Why can't you see the truth of it?" asked Mr. Russell, sighing for so many words wasted. "In that House by the Sea, who was your Secret Friend?"

"My Friend," said Jay, "is young and very full of youth. He is like a baby who knows life and yet finds it very amusing, and very new. He is without the gift of rest, but then he does not need it, the world in which he lives is not so tired and not so muddling as our world. In him my only belief and my only colour and my last dregs of romance, and certainly my youth survive. We never bother about reserve, and we never mind being sentimental in my Secret World. We just live, and we are never tortured by the futility of knowledge."

"Well," said Mr. Russell, "I had a Secret Friend in my House, and she was wonderful because she was so young that she knew nothing. She never asked questions, but she thought questions. She knew nothing, she was waiting to grow up. She had little colour, only peace and promise. I knew she would grow up, but I also knew she would never grow old. I knew she would learn much, but I also knew she would never become complete and ask no more questions. That voice of hers would always end on a questioning note. You see, I have found my Secret Friend, grown-up, grown old enough to enjoy and understand a new and more vital youth."

"Shall I find my Friend?" asked Jay.

"Yes," said Mr. Russell in a very low voice. "You can find him if you look. You can find him, grown very old and ugly and tired. There are different ways of growing up, and your Secret Friend was rash in using up too great a share of his sum of life in the House by the Sea."

Then Jay was suddenly enormously happy, and the veil of failure fell away from the day and from her life. She held in her hand incredible coincidences. The angle of the forest, the upright trees upon the sloping earth, the bend of the sky, the round bubble shapes of the clouds upon their appointed way, the agreement of the young leaves one with another, the unfailing pulse of the spring,—all these things seemed to

STELLA BENSON

her a chance, an unlikely and perfect consummation, that had been reached only by the extraordinary cleverness of God. All love and all success were pressed into a hair's-breadth, and yet the target was never missed.

"You shall go down to the House by the Sea," said Jay. "You shall go when the moon is next full over the sea that drowned our house. You shall come from the east, along the rocky path, as you used to come, between the foxgloves; you shall play at being a god, coming between the stars and the sea. And I will play at being a goddess, as I used to play at being a ghost, and I will run to meet you from the west, and the high grasses and the ferns shall whip my knees, and the thistles shall bow to me, and the sea shall be very calm and say no word, and there shall be no ship in sight. And we will go down the steep path to the shore, and we will stand where the sand is wet, and look up to where our drowned House used to be. And there shall be no facts any more, only the ghosts, and the dreams. Oh, surely it has never happened before—this meeting of Secret Friends—and surely no friend ever loved her friend as I love you, and surely there never was so little room for sin and disappointment in any love as there is in ours. Surely there are no tears in the world any more, and no Brown Borough, and no War. I don't care if I go hungry every day till we meet, I don't care if I have nothing but hated clothes to wear in my Secret World. I don't care if there are six changes on the journey to the sea, and at every change I miss my connection. I don't care if the end lasts only a minute, because the minute will last for ever, there are no facts any more. Because of you the little bothers of the world are gone, and the big bothers never did exist, because of you. Oh, I can say what I mean at last, and if it's nonsense—I don't care, because of you. . ."

Presently she said, "And now I wonder if I am very proud or very much ashamed of having spoken."

"You said once," Mr. Russell reminded her, "that life was just a bead upon a string. Well, does it much matter whether one bead is the colour of pride or the colour of shame? Does one successful bead more or less matter, my dear? I think it's all a succession of explanations, more or less lucid, and all different and all confusing. A string of beads more or less beautiful, and all unvalued. We don't know that any of the explanations are true, we don't know that any of the beads have any worth. We only know that they are ours. . ."

"I don't care if I trample my beads in the mud," said Jay. "Now let's go home and think."

When she and Chloris got home that evening to Eighteen Mabel Place, Chloris barked at a man who was waiting outside the door. He was a young man in khaki, with one star; he looked very white, and was reading something from his pocket-book.

"Great Scott, Bill," said Jay. "I thought you were busy sapping in France. Were you anywhere near Kew?"

I do not know if you will remember the name of young William Morgan. I think I have only mentioned him once or twice.

"I got back on leave two hours ago," said Mr. Morgan. "I have been waiting here thirty-two minutes. I saw Kew every day last week, and I was with him when he died, three hours before I came away yesterday."

Jay was silent. She opened the door, and in the sitting-room she placed—very carefully—two chairs looking at each other across the table.

"Jay," said William Morgan, "I am deadly afraid of doing this badly. Kew and I talked a good deal before it happened, and there was a good deal he wanted me to tell you. All the way back in the train and on the boat I have been writing notes to remind me what I had to say to you. I hope you don't mind. I hope you don't think it callous."

"No," said Jay.

"He was very anxious you should know the truth about it, because he said he had never lied to you. He was always sure that if he were shot it would be in the back while he was lacing his boots, or at some other unromantic moment. And in that case he said he could lie to Anonyma and your cousin vicariously through the War Office, which would write to them about Glory, and Duty, and Thanks Due. But he wanted me to write to you, and tell you how it happened, and tell you that death was just an ordinary old thing, no more romantic than anything else, without a capital letter, and that one died as one had lived—in a little ordinary way—and that there was no such thing as Glory between people who didn't lie to each other. I am telling you all this from my notes. I should never have thought of any of it for myself, as you know. I hope you don't mind."

"No," said Jay. She heard what he said, yet she was not listening. Her mind was listening to things heard a very long time ago. She heard herself and Kew in confidential chorus, saying those laboriously simple prayers that Anonyma used to teach them. She heard again the swishing that their feet used to make in the leaves of Kensington Gardens. Kew's was the louder swish by right. She thought of him as an admirable big brother of eight, with a round face and blunt feet and very hard hands. She heard the comfortable roar of the nursery fire, and the comfortable sound of autumn rain baffled by the window; she saw the early winter breakfast by lamplight, and the red nursery carpet that had an oblong track worn away round the table by the frequent game of "Little Men Jumping." She heard the voice of Kew clamouring against the voice of Nana because he would not eat his bacon-fat. On those days there was a horrid resurrection at luncheon of the bacon-fat uneaten at breakfast.

"As it happened," continued Mr. Morgan, no longer white, but very red, "he wasn't killed in an advance, or anything grand. He told me to tell you, so I am telling you. He was killed by a sniper while he was setting a trap of his own invention to catch the rats as they came over the parapet. He was shot in the chest very early yesterday morning, and he lived about four hours. He was not in much pain, he even laughed a little once or twice to think he should have lived and died so consistently. He told me that he had never seen a moment's real romantic fighting; he had never once felt patriotic or dramatic or dutiful, he said. He wandered a little, I think, because he seemed worried about the rats that might be caught in the trap he had set. He seemed to mix up the rats and the Boches. He said that these creatures didn't know they were vermin, they just thought they were honest average animals doing their bit, and then suddenly killed by a malignant chaos. My notes are very hurried. I am afraid I am repeating myself."

Jay remembered the mouse they once caught, and kept in a bottle for a day, and the palace they made for it out of stones and mud and moss, and the sun-bath of patted mud they made by the door of the palace. But the mouse, when it was installed, flashed straight out of the front door, and jumped the sun-bath, and knocked down a daisy, and was never seen again. But Jay and Kew used to believe that on moonlit nights it came back to the palace, and brought its wife and children, and was grateful to the palace builders.

"A few days before he was killed," said Mr. Morgan, "he told me that he had lied so successfully all his life that quite a lot of people thought him a most admirable young man. He said Anonyma once brought him into a book, and when he read that book he saw how lying paid, as long as one didn't lie to absolutely everybody. He said if he died Anonyma would write something very nice upon his memorial brass about a pure heart or everlasting life, and he thought you would smile a little at that. He said that he remembered going home with you in a 'bus and seeing on the window of the 'bus a text that promised everlasting life on certain conditions. He said the remembrance of that text tired him still. He said he had had too much of himself, he had known himself too well, and when death came, he wanted it to be an honest little death with no frills, and after that an everlasting sleep with no dreams. I am putting it all in the wrong order. I shall make you despise me. You talk so well yourself."

Jay was remembering the "Coos" they used to have in the big armchair in the nursery. When they found that they suddenly loved each other unbearably, they had a Coo, they tied themselves up in a little tangle together, and sang Coo in soft voices. And then they felt relieved. Jay remembered the last Coo. It happened when Kew's voice was breaking ten years ago, and he found that he could no longer coo except in a funny falsetto. So, rather than become farcical, the Coos ceased.

"I don't know quite why Kew wanted me to tell you all this," said Mr. Morgan, "except that he said you knew so much about him that you might as well get as near as possible to knowing everything. He never thought he would be killed, in fact I gave him a lot of messages of my own to give to my mother in case I went. But at the last, when he knew he was dying, he was desperately anxious you should know that he did not die a 'Stranger's death,' as he said. He thought any hint of drama about his death would spoil your friendship. He said you knew more than most people about friends, and he thought that in this way you could find for him a certain 'secret immortality' which would make the soil of France comfier for him to sleep in. And then he said, 'If I'm too poetic—like a swan—don't report me too accurately.' He seemed to go to sleep for some time after that, and every now and then he laughed very faintly in his sleep. I had to leave him for a bit, and when I came back he was still asleep. The only thing he said after that was: 'This is awfully exciting.' He said that about ten minutes before he died. I hope I'm not making it too painful for you, dear little Jay.'"

"No," said Jay. Quite irrelevantly, she had found her Secret Friend. She found a little dark wood, burnt and broken by fire, in a grey light, and there was a wet ditch that skirted the edge of it. She saw the hopeless and regretful sky, there was neither night nor morning in it, there was neither sun nor moon. These things she noticed, but more than all she saw her Secret Friend, lying crouched upon his side close to the ditch, with his arms about his face. She saw the slow leaves fall upon him from the ruined trees, she saw the damp air settle in beads upon his clothes. His feet were in the undergrowth, and above them the dripping net of the spider was flung. She had never seen her Friend quite still before. All her life her Secret Friend and her Secret Sea had kept her soul awake with movement. But her Friend was dead, and there was no more sea. The very fine rain blew across her Secret World, and blotted it out. The very distant sound of guns—which was not so much a sound as an indescribable vacuum of sound—shattered the walls of her bubble enchantment.

"Oh, darling Jay," said Mr. William Morgan, "I wish I could help you. I can't go away and leave you like this. I wish I could help you."

She found she had her forehead on the table, and her hands were knotted in her lap. And where once the Gate to the House had been, there was only London now. No more would the drum of the sea beat in her heart, there was nothing left but the throbbing of distant trams.

"So it's all lies. . ." she said quietly. "There really is a thing called death after all. People die. . ."

"Jay, darling, don't," sobbed Mr. Morgan. "For God's sake marry me, and I'll comfort you. I won't die—I swear I won't. And after all, it's Spring. There's no real death in the Spring. Kew can't have died."

"Oh, what's the use of these eternal seasons?" said Jay. "There is a thing called death. And death has no romance and no reason. The rats died, and Kew died, and the secret world died, and there is nothing left. . ."

It was young David, lord of sheep and cattle,
Pursued his Fate, the April fields among,
Singing a song of solitary battle,
A loud mad song, for he was very young.

Vivid the air—and something more than vivid,—
Tall clouds were in the sky—and something more,—
The light horizon of the spring was livid
With a steel smile that showed the teeth of War.

It was young David mocked the Philistine.
It was young David laughed beside the river.
There came his mother—his and yours and mine—
With five smooth stones, and dropped them in his quiver.

You never saw so green-and-gold a fairy.
You never saw such very April eyes.
She sang him sorrow's song to make him wary,
She gave him five smooth stones to make him wise.

The first stone is love, and that shall fail you.
The second stone is hate, and that shall fail you.
The third stone is knowledge, and that shall fail you.
The fourth stone is prayer, and that shall fail you.
The fifth stone shall not fail you.

For what is love, O lovers of my tribe?
And what is love, O women of my day?
Love is a farthing piece, a bloody bribe
Pressed in the palm of God, and thrown away.

And what is hate, O fierce and unforgiving?
And what shall hate achieve, when all is said?
A silly joke, that cannot reach the living,
A spitting in the faces of the dead.

And what is knowledge, O young men who tasted
The reddest fruit on that forbidden tree?

Knowledge is but a painful effort wasted,
A bitter drowning in a bitter sea.

And what is prayer, O waiters for the answer?
And what is prayer, O seekers of the cause?
Prayer is the weary soul of Herod's dancer,
Dancing before blind kings without applause.

The fifth stone is a magic stone, my David,
Made up of fear and failure, lies and loss.
Its heart is lead, and on its face is graved
A crooked cross, my son, a crooked cross.

It has no dignity to lend it value;
No purity—alas—it bears a stain.
You shall not give it gratitude, nor shall you
Recall it all your days except with pain.

Oh, bless your blindness, glory in your groping!
Mock at your betters with an upward chin!
And, when the moment has gone by for hoping,
Sling your fifth stone, O son of mine, and win.

Grief do I give you—grief and dreadful laughter.
Sackcloth for banner, ashes in your wine.
Go forth, go forth, nor ask me what comes after.
The fifth stone shall not fail you, son of mine.

GO FORTH, GO FORTH, AND SLAY THE PHILISTINE!

STELLA BENSON

There were a few very warm days and nights in the west last spring. It was at the time of the full moon.

There were so few clouds in the sky that when the sun went down it found no canvas on which to paint its picture. So it went down unpictured into a bank of grey heat that hid the horizon of the sea, and no one thought it worth watching except a man coming alone along the cliff from the northeast. The moon came up and filled the quarry with ghosts, and with confused and blinded memories. The sea advanced in armies of great smooth waves, but under the moon the wind went down, and the waves went down, and there was less and less sound in the air.

One man watched the dwindling waves troop into the cove near the quarry. There was only one pair of eyes in the whole world that tried that night to trace in the air the shape of a drowned house. There was only one shadow by the quarry for the moon to cast upon the thyme. There was no voice but the voice of the sea. No passing but the peaceful passing of the lambs disturbed the thistles and the foxgloves.

The sea rose like a wall across the night, a wall that shut half of life away. The sky fell like a curtain on the land, but there was no piece to be played, so the curtain was never raised.

One man waited all the night through, like a child waiting for the fairies. The sea grew calmer and calmer, the tide went down, and the cove spread out its long sands like fingers into the sea. There was a shadow on the sands below the quarry, and it may have been the shadow of a house. And perhaps when the tide came up at dawn it devoured old footprints upon the shore, the prints of feet that will never come back. I think that when the moon fled away into oblivion, it was not only the moon that fled, but also a bubble world, full of dead secrets.

How foolish to wait for the culmination of a secret story! How foolish of a man to wait all night for the redemption of an old promise, for the resurrection of a forgotten romance! There are no secret stories, there is no secret world, there are no secret friends. The House by the Sea has been drowned, and even its ghosts have forgotten it. After all, there was nothing to remember. The gate to the House is barred, not by a lock but by a laugh. Reality and not adversity has blown the bubble away.

I remember the moment when Jay found four-fifths of her life proved false. I remember that she besieged the world with tears; I remember that she bruised her hands against the iron gate. How foolish to bruise one's hands against nothingness!

Anti-Climax

"It is well," sighed Anonyma, "that our little Jay has at last found Romance. Since first she came to my arms—a toddling sceptic of four—I have seen what she lacked, I have prayed that I—who possessed it—might perhaps be inspired to give her the Clue. . . Yet to young Bill Morgan it was given to show her the way. . . to unlock the door. . . Oh! Russ, we grow older and wiser and are left behind. The young reap where we have sown. . . Is this always to be the end of our youth?"

Mr. Russell laughed a little. "Yes," he said. "This is the end."

The finest fruit God ever made
Hangs from the Tree of Heaven blue.
It hangs above the steel sea blade
That cuts the world's great globe in two.

The keenest eye that ever saw
Stares out of Heaven into mine,
Spins out my heart, and seems to draw
My soul's elastic very fine.

The greatest beacon ever fired
Stands up on Heaven's Hill to show
The limit of the thing desired
Beyond which man may never go.

*　　*　　*　　*　　*

At midnight, when the night did dance
Along the hours that led to morning,
I saw a little boat advance
Towards the great moon's beacon warning.

(The moon, God's Slave, who lights the torch,
Lest men should slip between the bars,
And run aground on Heav'n and scorch
To death upon a bank of stars.)

The little boat, on leaning keel,
Sang up the mountains of the sea,
Bearing a man who hoped to steal
God's Slave from out eternity.

My love, I see you through my tears.
No pity in your face I see.
I have sailed far across the years:
Stretch out, stretch out your arms to me.

My love, I have an island seen,
So shadowed, God's most piercing star

Shall never see where we have been,
Shall never whisper where we are.

There we will wander, you and I,
Down guilty and delightful ways,
While palm-trees plait their fingers high
Against your God's enormous gaze.

For oh—the joy of two and two,
Your Paradise shall never see
The ecstasy of me and you,
The white delight of you and me.

I know the penalty—the clutch
Of God's great rocks upon my keel.
Drowned in the ocean of Too Much—
So ends your thief—yet let me steal. . .

The Slave of God she froze her face,
The Slave of God she paid no heed,
And thund'ring down high Heaven's space
Loud angels mocked the sailor's greed.

The diamond sun arose, and tossed
A billion gems across the sea.
"The Slave of God is lost, is lost,
The Slave of God is lost to me. . ."

He grounded on the common beach,
He trod the little towns of men,
And God removed from his reach
The cup of Heaven's passion then,
And gave him vulgar love and speech,
And gave him threescore years and ten.

STELLA BENSON

A Note About the Author

Stella Benson (1892–1933) was an English feminist poet, travel writer, and novelist. Born into a wealthy Shropshire family, Benson was the niece of bestselling novelist Mary Cholmondeley. Educated from a young age, she lived in London, Germany, and Switzerland in her youth, which was marked by her parents' acrimonious separation. As a young woman in London, she became active in the women's suffrage movement, which informed her novels *This Is the End* (1917) and *Living Alone* (1919). In 1918, Benson traveled to the United States, settling in Berkley for a year and joining the local Bohemian community. In 1920, she met her husband in China and began focusing on travel writing with such essay collections and memoirs as *The Little World* (1925) and *World Within Worlds* (1928). Benson, whose work was admired by Virginia Woolf, continued publishing novels, stories, and poems until her death from pneumonia in the Vietnamese province of Tonkin.

A Note from the Publisher

Spanning many genres, from non-fiction essays to literature classics to children's books and lyric poetry, Mint Edition books showcase the master works of our time in a modern new package. The text is freshly typeset, is clean and easy to read, and features a new note about the author in each volume. Many books also include exclusive new introductory material. Every book boasts a striking new cover, which makes it as appropriate for collecting as it is for gift giving. Mint Edition books are only printed when a reader orders them, so natural resources are not wasted. We're proud that our books are never manufactured in excess and exist only in the exact quantity they need to be read and enjoyed.

bookfinity™

Discover more of your favorite classics with Bookfinity™.

- Track your reading with custom book lists.
- Get great book recommendations for your personalized Reader Type.
- Add reviews for your favorite books.
- AND MUCH MORE!

Visit **bookfinity.com** and take the fun Reader Type quiz to get started.

Enjoy our classic and modern companion pairings!

Classic & Modern

Printed in the USA
CPSIA information can be obtained
at www.ICGtesting.com
JSHW080000150824
68134JS00020B/2183

9 781513 291161